Previous Manny Rivera Mysteries by Rich Curtin:

Artifacts of Death

February's Files

Trails of Deception

MoonShadow Murder

Deadly Games

Death Saint

Author's Website:

www.richcurtinnovels.com

# THE SHAMAN'S SECRET

A MANNY RIVERA MYSTERY

RICH CURTIN

ISBN: 1976216680
ISBN-13: 9781976216688
Library of Congress Control Number: 2017914651
CreateSpace Independent Publishing Platform
North Charleston, South Carolina
Printed in the United States of America

# ACKNOWLEDGEMENTS

I am indebted to Kay Laird, Sheryleen Grothus, Rebecca Brown, and Diane Evans for reviewing the manuscript of this book and making valuable suggestions for improving the writing and the story. My sincerest thanks to each of them.

# 1

DEPUTY SHERIFF MANNY RIVERA was in an upbeat mood as he cruised through the curves of Highway 128 alongside the Colorado River. The massive red rock walls on each side of the river glowed a shimmering copper color as an early November sun rose in a clear blue sky. The tourist season was winding down and the need for law enforcement actions was dwindling—and that suited him just fine. He was hopeful things would stay that way. Gloria Valdez would be arriving from New Mexico in three days and he didn't want anything to interfere with his plans for spending a couple of fun days with her. The buzzing of his cell phone interrupted his thoughts.

The caller was Millie Ives, the sheriff's dispatcher. Rivera had learned years ago that when she called him by cell phone instead of police-band radio, it was a sensitive and serious matter that she didn't wish to share with the hundreds of Moab civilians who owned police scanners. He instantly feared his plans for Gloria's visit were in jeopardy.

"Manny, a Moab local by the name of James Kirtland just called and reported a shooting out in the Big Triangle. One man seriously wounded. An EMS unit from Grand Junction has been dispatched. Kirtland said he believes the shooting was deliberate. The Dolores River is running low enough so you'll be able to drive across the gravel bar at Roberts Bottom." She gave him the GPS coordinates of the crime scene and directions for navigating the dirt roads which would lead him to the general vicinity. Beyond that, he would have to proceed on foot. Rivera knew he was headed for some of the most remote backcountry in southeast Utah.

He made a U-turn, switched on the light bar of his Grand County Sheriff's Department pickup truck, and sped upriver toward the Dewey Bridge. He knew Kirtland from playing in pick-up basketball games at the high school gym. He was tall, mid-twenties, a good athlete, and quiet. "What makes Kirtland think it was deliberate?"

"He said there were four of them patrolling the area, looking for the perps who have been poaching bighorn sheep out there for the past year or so. He said the victim called him twice by cell phone—once to say he thought he'd heard a gunshot in the small canyon he was exploring, and a second time to say he'd been shot and needed help. Kirtland arrived on the scene about ten minutes ago. The other two are on their way."

"I'm guessing they're all members of that vigilante group I've been hearing about—the ones threatening revenge against the bighorn poachers."

"That is correct. I go to the same church as Kirtland's grandmother. She talked to me one Sunday about James. Said she was worried because he'd joined some radical militia group dedicated to preventing human destruction of the environment. They call themselves *The Keepers of Order.* They claim the authorities are doing nothing about the bighorn poaching, so they intend to take care of the problem themselves. She was visibly upset."

"I'm nearly at the Dewey Bridge."

"I'll call the Bureau of Land Management and notify Adam Dunne of the shooting."

Rivera clicked off and turned right on a gravel road just before the bridge. He slammed the palm of his hand against the steering wheel, knowing he would now be involved in an investigation during Gloria's visit. So much for all his careful planning. He thought about calling her and postponing the visit, but he missed her and wanted to be with her. This was going to be a problem—whenever he was working on a case involving a capital crime, he felt duty bound to work twenty-four seven until it was solved. What would he do with Gloria?

Rivera had occasion to visit the Big Triangle only once before. It was during a case involving drug runners growing marijuana on BLM land. The Big Triangle, referred to by locals as the Dolores Triangle, was a rugged and remote area of Utah cut off from the rest of the state by the Colorado and Dolores Rivers. It was 200 square miles of mostly unpopulated mesas, canyons, sagebrush flats, and rocky bluffs, so there was rarely a reason for a deputy to go there. There were no bridges over either river connecting the Big Triangle to the rest of Utah. Driving across the Dolores River when it was running low, or circling around through Colorado, a drive of nearly a hundred miles, were the only means of access. It reminded Rivera of the sign which now-retired Deputy L.D. Mincey used to keep in his office: *The Big Triangle—You Can't Get There From Here.*

The gravel road transitioned to dirt and, after a couple of jolting miles, Rivera arrived at the Dolores River. He drove across the gravel bar and headed upriver along a primitive road which, after a distance of three miles, turned north and wound its way up a series of switchbacks to the top of Hotel Mesa. From there, he drove on the dirt of BLM Route 109 across the high mesa until it transitioned to BLM Route 107.

After twenty miles of bouncing along the rutted back road, he passed the entrance to the McGinty Ranch on his left. There the road abruptly turned east. A quarter mile farther, he turned left onto a two-track which, after a few hundred yards, dead-ended at a rock field. Rivera strapped on his daypack and followed a barely visible trail which wound through rocks large enough to dwarf a human. Soon, the terrain began sloping upward as he entered the mouth of a canyon bracketed by red rock walls 200 feet high. Using his GPS receiver to guide him to the crime scene coordinates, he wound his way through pinyon pine, juniper, and cottonwoods until he arrived at a clearing where he spotted a young man lying on the ground. James Kirtland was standing next to him, holding a rifle at his side. Both Kirtland and the victim were wearing camouflage outfits.

"Manny, I'm so glad you're here. But where are the medics?"

"James, lay the rifle on the ground and step back."

"Huh? I didn't shoot him, Manny. I'm the one who called and reported it."

"I know James, but this is a crime scene." He raised his voice slightly, articulating each word. "Lay the rifle down now and stand over there." He pointed to a pinyon pine about fifteen feet from the victim.

Kirtland placed the rifle on the ground. "Sure, Manny. No problem." He backed up to the tree, holding his hands partway up with a wide-eyed look of disbelief on his face.

"I'm going to have to pat you down, James. It's procedure. Just stand still." Rivera walked around behind him and frisked him, removing a hunting knife from a sheath on his belt and tossing it next to the rifle.

"Manny, you don't think—"

"No, I don't, James. Just bear with me." Rivera walked over to the victim, knelt at his side, and checked his condition. He had a serious chest wound, up high on his right side. Rivera felt for a pulse—the man was still alive. The deputy removed his daypack, extracted a tube of antibiotic ointment, some gauze pads, and some adhesive tape. He cut open the man's shirt with his pocketknife, applied the ointment, and covered the wound with gauze pads. There were powder burns on the front of the man's shirt indicating he was shot at close range. Rivera gently checked the victim's back for an exit wound, finding none—the bullet had lodged itself somewhere within his body. Rivera realized nothing more could be done until the medics arrived. He hoped they wouldn't get lost trying to find the place.

Rivera looked up at Kirtland. "What's his name?"

"Zeke Stanton. He's new to Moab. Is he still alive?"

"He's alive. The medics should be here shortly. I understand you were out here looking for those bighorn sheep poachers."

"That's right."

"Who else was with you?"

"There were four of us. Zeke and me and Butch Jeffers and Butch's younger brother Billy. Butch is our leader. We were spread out in half-mile intervals between here and the Colorado River, heading northeast. We'd gotten a tip that the poachers were in the area."

"I understand you're members of a militia."

"We're not supposed to comment on that, but yeah, we are." He smiled. It was obvious he was proud to be a member.

"What were you going to do if you found the poachers?"

"Make a citizen's arrest and bring them in."

"How did you know the poachers would be out here today?"

"Like I said, we got a tip."

"Who gave you the tip?"

"He wants to remain anonymous for his own safety."

Rivera considered that. Decided not to press the matter. "Where are the other members of your group?"

"They're headed this way. This is pretty rough country so it'll take them awhile longer to get here."

Minutes later, just as two medics trotted into the area carrying a stretcher, a young man wearing a camouflage outfit and carrying a rifle, appeared from an opening between a large chunk of fallen red rock and a copse of junipers. He was tall and lanky with a bewildered expression on his face. Rivera figured he couldn't be more than seventeen years old—too young to be playing in this kind of game. He instructed the young man to lay down his rifle. The boy complied, after which Rivera frisked him, removing a small caliber pistol from the pocket of his jacket. Rivera recognized him as Billy Jeffers, the son of one of the Grand County commissioners. Jeffers, who couldn't take his eyes off his wounded friend, walked over and stood next to Kirtland.

While the medics attended to Stanton, the fourth member of the militia, also carrying a rifle, arrived at the scene. Rivera recognized him as Butch Jeffers, Billy's older brother by about twelve years. He had a reputation around Moab as a trouble-maker—not a lawbreaker, but a bully and an intimidator. He was wearing a camouflage outfit with an ammo belt draped across his shoulder. He was a large man and stood about six-feet-two inches tall, about three inches taller than Rivera. He strode up to Rivera. "What happened here?" he demanded.

"Put your rifle on the ground and turn around," ordered Rivera.

"Like hell I will. What happened to Zeke?"

"Lay the rifle down now."

Butch looked Rivera up and down. Smirked.

"Do what he says, Butch," yelled Kirtland.

"Shut up, James. This is none of your business."

Rivera stepped toward Butch who reacted by raising his rifle. Rivera grabbed Butch's wrist, twisted it with both hands, and threw him to the ground face down. Rivera put a knee on his back and cuffed him. He collected the rifle and set it aside. Then he frisked Butch, finding a 9-millimeter handgun in his pocket.

"You idiot," shouted Butch. "Don't you know who I am?" He spit dead grass and dirt out of his mouth. "I'll have your job for this."

The medics, now finished administering to Zeke Stanton's wound, placed him on the stretcher. "You okay here?" said one of them to Rivera as they were leaving.

"I'm fine. See if you can save that boy."

The medics carted Stanton off just as Adam Dunne, the local BLM Investigative Agent and a good friend of Rivera's, arrived at the scene. "Need help?" he asked Rivera.

He pointed to Butch. "Keep an eye on this one. I need to tag all these weapons before I forget which is which."

Butch rolled over and struggled to sit up. "If you guys had been doing your goddamn jobs, none of this would have happened."

"What do you mean?" asked Dunne.

"Bighorn poaching has been going on out here for a year and you law enforcement people have done nothing about it."

"There are only a few of us covering several million acres. We do what we can. We can't stake out the whole backcountry." Dunne sounded defensive.

"You guys are next to worthless. And take these damn cuffs off me."

"Not just yet." said Rivera.

"I'll tell you one thing," said Butch through clenched teeth. "Those poachers aren't going to get away with shooting Zeke. There's going to be hell to pay for this. From now on, this is war."

# 2

THE FOLLOWING MORNING, Rivera sat in his office poring over maps of the Big Triangle and trying to push out of his mind the disappointment he felt that his plans for Gloria's visit had been ruined. The day hikes through geologic wonderlands and dinners at Moab's finest restaurants would have to wait for another time. He was studying the road system and the general topology of the landscape, trying to formulate a mental picture of this unfamiliar part of the backcountry.

The dust had settled from the previous day's events. Zeke Stanton was in the Grand Junction Community Hospital in critical but stable condition. A .38 caliber bullet had been removed from his chest and forwarded to Rivera by messenger. James Kirtland and Billy Jeffers had been released yesterday evening after questioning and sent home. Butch Jeffers was cooling his heels in a county jail cell.

Rivera's challenge seemed clear—find and apprehend the men who were poaching bighorn sheep in the Big Triangle. One of them had shot Stanton and he would be charged with either attempted murder or murder, depending upon whether Stanton survived his wound. The others would be charged with hunting bighorns without a permit, conspiracy to commit a felony, and anything else Rivera could come up with that would stick. As far as the militia members were concerned, Rivera would keep an eye on them. As long as they didn't harm anyone or interfere with his investigation, he'd have to let them play their silly but dangerous games. Hopefully Butch Jeffers and his three cohorts had learned a lesson yesterday, but deep down, Rivera knew that was just wishful thinking.

The door to Rivera's office was thrown open, slamming against the wall, as Sheriff Denny Campbell strode in. He was an imposing man in his mid-fifties, six feet four inches tall with broad shoulders and a salt-and-pepper buzz cut. He was wearing his perpetual frown.

"Rivera, are you crazy? Why the hell did you lock up Butch Jeffers?" he bellowed.

Rivera, having become accustomed to Campbell's boorish decorum by now, replied in a calm matter-of-fact tone of voice. "He failed to follow orders at a crime scene. Got belligerent. It was necessary."

"Well I released him. Don't you know his father is a county councilman?"

"Sure, I knew that."

"Did you also know that the general election is next week and that his father is one of my biggest supporters?

I'm running for reelection, you know. I don't need this kind of problem right now."

Rivera shrugged. He wasn't planning on filing charges against Butch Jeffers. He just wanted to teach him some manners and was going to release him in a few hours. Rivera knew Andrew Jeffers was Campbell's golfing buddy and political supporter, but his son Butch was a troublemaker in Moab and needed to be taught some respect for people. Rivera stared passively at Campbell without answering his question.

Twenty seconds passed. The silence seemed to make Campbell uneasy. "Well, carry on," he said as he turned and left the office.

Rivera sat back and shook his head. He mused about how much more enjoyable his professional life would be if Campbell lost the election. Campbell had been a royal pain in the butt since becoming sheriff. Leroy Bradshaw, the former sheriff and Rivera's revered mentor, had decided to drop out of the race for reelection after his wife succumbed to cancer. Too many memories in Moab, he'd said. That left Campbell as the only remaining candidate in the race, and he won in an uncontested election. He was a retired street cop from Detroit and knew nothing about the ways of a small town and its people. He was unqualified to be sheriff and seemed to have little real interest in the job. Golfing with his buddies took up most of his time. His opponent in the upcoming election was a fifty-one-year-old retired Army colonel by the name of Louise Anderson. Rivera had met her once about a year ago in connection with a fundraiser for the Moab Home for Needy Children. She'd struck him as a caring and strong individual. Rivera had been encouraged by many in town to run for the office himself, but the thought of spending each day mired down in political and administrative chores left him cold. Criminal investigations were his passion.

He returned his attention to the topo maps on his desk. They gave him a large-picture overview of the Big Triangle's geography. He supplemented the maps with satellite photos from Google Maps to help fill in the surface details. The sector of interest was the rocky terrain between the Colorado River and Marble Canyon. It was an area of small mesas crosscut with a myriad of canyons. Staking out the area would be futile—it was too large and too broken for one man or even several to do much good. Besides, he had an intense dislike of stakeouts. They seemed to be the least sensible way to approach an investigation and, he believed, were to be used only as a last resort. He was searching his mind for a better idea—a logical one—when Adam Dunne entered his office. A BLM Investigative Agent for over twenty years, Dunne had worked with Rivera on several cases since Rivera's arrival in Moab six years ago. Dunne closed the office door and slumped into one of the visitor's chairs.

"Heck of a way to start the weekend," said Dunne.

"I know. Bad timing all around. Gloria's arriving Monday evening."

"Man, this bighorn poaching business is stirring up a hornet's nest. The BLM is getting a ton of pressure from environmental groups and animal rights people demanding we put an end to it immediately. And yesterday's shooting has brought even more attention to the problem. This morning, we started getting calls from Washington. The politicians are circling, sensing an opportunity to win some votes. Trouble is, the chance of catching the poachers is somewhere between slim and none."

Rivera nodded. "Yeah. I've been sitting here trying to figure out where to start an investigation, but so far I'm drawing a blank. Problem is, I'm not very familiar with the Big Triangle and I don't know the first thing about bighorn poaching." Rivera drew a circle on the map with his finger. "This is the general area where Stanton was shot. How familiar are you with the Big Triangle?"

"I've been through there a few times over the years. It's a huge, barren area with a few dirt roads left over from early mineral exploration days. Mostly rugged and broken country. The vast majority of it is BLM land but there are also a few privately-owned ranches here and there." He stood up and studied the map. "As I remember it, there are two ranches near the place where Stanton was shot. One is the Alvin McGinty Ranch which runs west from his front gate over to the Colorado River. McGinty raises beef cattle on a few thousand acres. The other ranch is small and a little farther east. It's home to the Center for Cosmic Consciousness. I've never visited the place but it's supposed to be some kind of retreat venue where people go to find contentment in their lives."

Rivera smiled. "Contentment sounds pretty good right now. Maybe I should sign up."

Dunne laughed. "They don't admit hopeless cases. And besides, working for Sheriff Campbell wouldn't leave much room for contentment."

"I won't comment on that."

Dunne lowered his voice. "Maybe Tuesday's election will solve that problem for you."

"We'll see. Sheriff Campbell has been spending a lot of time campaigning and he's pretty confident he'll win. Says he doesn't think anyone will vote for a woman to become sheriff."

"From what I'm hearing around town, he might be wrong."

"Really?" Rivera was surprised at that, but he wasn't comfortable discussing the subject with anyone, not even a close friend like Dunne. As much as he disliked and disrespected Campbell, he didn't want to display any disloyalty—not because of any concern for Campbell, but because it would reflect badly on the entire Sheriff's Department. He tapped the map with his index finger. "Any idea why the poachers are operating in this particular area? Are there a lot of bighorns around there?"

"I read a report on our district's bighorn program awhile back. If I remember right, there are two herds in that part of the Big Triangle—a total of maybe a hundred and twenty animals. Despite a repopulation program by the BLM, the number of animals in those herds has been decreasing due to poaching. During the past year or so, several decapitated ram carcasses have been found in the area, and a few rams seem to have disappeared altogether. I don't remember all the details but we have an expert on our staff who can educate you on all that. He's the project manager in charge of their health and well-being for this district. Name's John Singleton. He has degrees in animal husbandry and range management. If you want to learn more about the bighorns, he's definitely the go-to guy."

Ten minutes later, Rivera entered the BLM Field Office building on Dogwood Avenue. The staff members working there were responsible for overseeing the nearly two million acres of canyon country wilderness surrounding Moab. He found Singleton's office, knocked on the open door, and introduced himself. Singleton was a pleasant looking, wiry man of average height who appeared to be in his mid-forties. His light brown hair was thinning on top and his shirtsleeves were rolled up. His desk was covered with charts and maps, and he had the appearance of a busy man. Coffee was offered and accepted and, after some small talk, Rivera got down to business.

"Have you heard about the shooting we had out in the Big Triangle yesterday?"

He nodded. "Adam filled me in."

"It looks like the shooter might be one of the bighorn poachers who have been operating out there. If I can find the poachers and apprehend them, maybe I'll have my shooter. Trouble is, I don't know where to start looking. I'm hoping you can help educate me on the bighorns and the way poachers operate."

Singleton's expression turned grim. "Bighorns in this district are my responsibility. My job is to monitor the herds, increase their population, and improve their health. Unfortunately during the past year, we've lost seven bighorn rams that we're aware of. It's very frustrating. We've worked hard to build up the herds, and then these lowlifes come along and kill the animals or steal them. I'm glad you're getting involved and I'll be happy to educate you. Any place in particular you'd like me to start?"

"Let's start with the poaching itself. What would motivate people to poach bighorn sheep?"

"Well, the short answer, of course, is money. In your work, I'm sure you've seen bighorns in the backcountry from time to time."

"Sure, but only from a distance."

"The bighorn sheep we have in southern Utah are called desert bighorns. Adults are generally about five feet long and stand about three feet high. The rams can weigh as much as 280 pounds. At full adulthood, their massive horns curl around a full 360 degrees. They are gorgeous animals, iconic in the red rock canyon country. Unfortunately, their stoic beauty is what makes them targets for poachers."

"I didn't realize they were that big. From a distance, they look about the same size as domestic sheep."

"Oh, no. They're much larger. And way more nimble. They have no trouble trotting along a one-inch ledge on an otherwise sheer bluff. Anyway, it's the rams that hunters prize. Nearly every hunter would like to have a bighorn ram's head mounted on his wall. Trouble is, legal hunting tags are almost impossible to come by. They're issued on a lottery basis and only a few hunters are lucky enough to be selected each year, so a hunter has only a tiny chance of getting one even if he enters the lottery every year of his life. Sometimes, states will auction off a tag or two to raise funds. One time, a hunter from New York bid $300,000 to get a Montana tag. That gives you some idea of the money involved in poaching. Because the legal tags are so scarce, a certain amount of poaching has historically taken place in the West. Normally it's rare, but recently the poaching in the Big Triangle has stepped up dramatically."

"Why do you suppose the poachers are operating in that particular area?"

"Probably because it's remote and unpopulated. There's a far smaller chance of being seen, much less apprehended by the authorities. It's all rough country, mostly steep bluffs, rocky canyons, and talus slopes. The heartbreaking part is that the area around Star Canyon is one we've been working hard to repopulate."

"Repopulate? Why was it necessary to repopulate?"

"The original herds disappeared long ago. Back in the 1960s, there were no bighorn sheep in that area at all. In recent years, we transplanted rams and ewes from the San Juan River canyon to the Big Triangle in an attempt to establish new herds there. And we've been pretty successful doing it. But the recent poaching has been a real setback for us."

"But why did you choose that particular area?"

"The terrain looked like a perfect habitat for bighorns. It had the right geology—lots of rocky areas with steep cliffs and rugged outcroppings. Mountain lions are the greatest fear of the bighorns, so they prefer sheer cliffs where they can escape. They can run up and down cliffs effortlessly, whereas a mountain lion generally won't risk navigating that kind of terrain. We also know that a thousand or more years ago, there were lots of bighorns in the area."

"How do you know that?"

"From the petroglyphs and pictographs left on canyon walls by the Fremont people. The depictions are unmistakable—rectangular bodies, stick legs, and heads with curlicue horns. The bighorns had to have been there or those glyphs wouldn't have been inscribed on the rocks."

"So how did you go about repopulating the area?"

"We selected certain bighorns from the population along the San Juan River corridor, used tranquilizer darts to immobilize them, and then transported them by helicopter to the Big Triangle."

Rivera considered the cost of such an operation. A lot of money and effort had been expended to transport each animal. "Are the bighorns an endangered species?"

"Not endangered, but their numbers are low. There used to be millions of them in North America. Now, in Utah, we're down to about two thousand desert bighorns."

"What would poachers have to do to get their hands on a bighorn ram?"

"Sometimes they simply shoot the animal in the wild and decapitate it. They carry the head back to their pickup, load it in the bed with a tarp over it, and take off. Sell the head to someone who wants to mount it on a damn wall. Other times, the poachers capture the rams alive and sell them to one of those exotic game hunting ranches."

"I've heard of those hunting ranches but I'm not familiar with them."

"They're located all over the Southwest, many of them in Texas. Typically, they're thousands of acres in size with a high fence around the perimeter. The owners stock them with exotic animals and hunters pay large fees to hunt and shoot an animal. The ranches also provide taxidermy services and arrange for transportation. There's a lot of money involved so hunters are housed in plush quarters and served gourmet meals and fine liquor by an attentive staff. A hunter goes out, locates the animal he wants to shoot, and kills it at long range with a high-powered rifle. Most of the hunting that goes on at those ranches is within the law. It usually involves axis deer or aoudad sheep or some other legal species. But sometimes, a hunter will offer to pay big money to a ranch operator for a chance to bag a bighorn. So some of the operators—the shady ones—will pay a poacher for a live bighorn and turn it loose on the ranch for a hunter to stalk and kill. All that's illegal of course. Everyone involved is breaking the law."

"How would the poachers go about capturing an animal?"

"Same way we do. Bighorn sheep are rather docile. They'll keep their distance but they don't sprint off like a deer at the first sight of a human being. So you can get close enough to fire a tranquilizing dart and temporarily disable an animal. If a road is nearby, the animal can be transported out by vehicle. If not, a small helicopter can be used."

"A helicopter would be expensive. How much would one of those hunting ranches pay for a live ram?"

"You'd be surprised. On the black market, a live, full grown ram could easily bring fifty thousand dollars. Probably more."

Rivera whistled. He sat back, thinking. There was far more profit in bighorn poaching than he'd realized. "So if the poachers wanted a live animal, they would first have to locate it and then go through the same process you do when you relocate an animal."

"That's correct."

"How would they locate a bighorn ram in the wild?"

"I'm not sure exactly how they're doing it, but they've been damn effective at finding them. Let me get Charlie Baxter in here. He's my electronics technician. Animal tracking has become kind of high tech, so Charlie helps me with that end of the business. He can explain it a lot better than I can."

Singleton got up and headed out of his office. He stopped at the door and whispered back to Rivera. "Charlie's a great employee but sometimes it's a little hard to follow what he's talking about. He jumps all over the place. And he might bowl you over with technical terms, so be prepared."

Rivera glanced around Singleton's office while he waited. It was a small office with a gray metal desk, a matching table, and six chairs. The walls were covered with photographs of bighorn ewes, lambs, and rams, Singleton's framed college degrees, topo maps of the surrounding area, and an honorary certificate from the Wildlife Conservation Society. On the desk was a photograph of Singleton, a woman Rivera assumed was his wife, and three young children.

Singleton returned with Charlie Baxter, a man in his twenties who could have doubled for a young Paul Simon. Singleton made the introductions and sat down behind his desk. Baxter pulled a chair over to where Rivera was sitting and placed it so that he was directly facing the deputy. He leaned forward with an enthusiastic expression that suggested he couldn't wait to start explaining things.

"I'm interested in the whole animal tracking business—how it works and what kind of equipment is involved," said Rivera.

Baxter grinned and didn't miss a beat. "So, we start by putting tracking collars on the lead animals in each herd. Did John tell you we track herds all over southeast Utah? We have herds in Canyonlands National Park, Arches National Park, Capitol Reef, Cedar Mesa, down along the San Juan River, and—"

Singleton raised his hand. "Deputy Rivera doesn't need to hear all that, Charlie. Just tell him about the tracking."

Rivera tried not to smile. Just as Singleton had said, Baxter had a hard time staying on topic.

"Right. So we locate the ram we want to collar. Sometimes we collar ewes but that's another story. We get close, fire a tranquilizing dart, then run to the animal so it doesn't roll down an incline or off a cliff. We want to be sure the animal doesn't end up injured or crippled. We fasten the collar and stay with the animal until we're sure it's okay. Each collar contains a GPS receiver and a micro-computer that keeps a record of the animal's route during the day. I've programmed our collars to transmit the tracking data once every twelve hours. The information goes up to a satellite and is relayed over the internet to our computers. That way, we have a continuous record of a herd's movements and by inference, its health. If we're out near the herd, I can access the data in my office computer via cell phone. In the old days, we had to use a handheld transceiver and antenna to receive the signals."

Rivera wanted to ask a question about the handheld transceivers but Baxter kept talking.

"The technology is so cool. The collars send out pulse code modulated signals on an FM carrier..."

Singleton interrupted again. "Just a second, Charlie. Do you have a question, Deputy Rivera?"

"I'm guessing the poachers aren't set up to receive data from a satellite, so I was wondering how hard it would be for them to get their hands on one of those handheld transceivers."

"I see where you're going," said Baxter. "Anyone can buy a transceiver and an antenna on the internet, but I set up the system so that the transmitted data is encrypted. So even if the poachers were able to pick up the signal, they still wouldn't have access to the GPS coordinates." He thought for a long moment. "I guess it's possible they might be able to triangulate on the carrier signal, although in that rugged terrain out there, it wouldn't be easy."

"But it could be done?" asked Rivera.

Baxter's smile faded. He took off his glasses, chewed on the tip, and frowned. "It *is* possible."

"We've known about the poaching in the Big Triangle for about a year," said Singleton. "At least four rams are missing. One was wearing a collar. We also found three headless ram carcasses out there— animals shot and then decapitated. That's a total of seven. It wouldn't surprise me if there were more that we haven't discovered yet."

"What have you done about it?"

Singleton shrugged. "I reported it to Adam and he called a friend of his who's an FBI agent in the Salt

Lake City office. The poaching episodes are crimes committed on federal land, so the FBI has jurisdiction. Adam wasn't able to get much help, though. His friend said they had their hands full with more serious crimes—things like terrorism and bank fraud. Poaching isn't high on their list of priorities. There's not much Charlie and I can do. We're not trained in law enforcement. And Adam's all by himself. His law enforcement responsibilities cover all of southeast Utah, an area the size of Maryland."

"Since the poachers shot a man in Grand County, it's now the sheriff's business too," said Rivera. "Hopefully we can help."

# 3

RIVERA EXITED THE BLM building realizing the poachers were more than just a few amateurs trying to make a quick buck. There was a lot of money involved and that meant they could justify tracking equipment for locating the herds and a helicopter for transporting them. He adjusted his thinking, now understanding he was up against a well-organized, highly experienced operation consisting of people willing to kill anyone who got in their way.

Rivera knew he would have to return to the Big Triangle to continue his investigation. Adam Dunne had said the McGinty Ranch and the Center for Cosmic Consciousness held the only residents living in the area. Maybe McGinty or somebody at the Center had seen something that would be helpful, but before visiting them, Rivera wanted to learn something about the people who lived there.

There was no better source for that kind of intelligence than Chris Carey, a retired newspaper journalist and friend who lived in Moab. Rivera recalled Carey once mentioning he was writing a feature article on the Center, so maybe he could supply some useful information. He was an award-winning investigative journalist who had spent his career working for various Utah newspapers. Unfortunately, he'd been forced to retire eight years ago due to cutbacks in the newspaper industry stemming from internet competition. Since his retirement, he'd assisted Rivera on several cases, providing invaluable information and insights. Then, four months ago, Carey's wife passed away. Rivera knew he was beset with grief and the helpless feeling that his life was inexorably winding down. Maybe he would welcome the opportunity to work with Rivera on a case once again.

When the front door of Carey's home opened, Rivera saw an unshaven, pale, dispirited-looking version of Carey's former self. He was in his late sixties, medium height, with a friendly face and a few wisps of white hair on his head. He was wearing a bathrobe and socks. Carey had lost a lot of weight since the last time Rivera saw him, but the old newspaper man managed a grin.

"C'mon in, Manny. It's great to see you."

They settled into leather chairs in Carey's den, a place where they'd had many conversations over the years, usually concerning one of Rivera's ongoing investigations.

"How are you doing, Chris?"

"I'm okay. I just miss Rita. I'm kind of lost without her. I need something challenging to keep my mind busy so I'm not just sitting around the house all day feeling sorry for myself. I'm hoping you've brought me a problem to work on."

"Well, I do have a problem, Chris. And I could use some help." Rivera noticed Carey's face light up. The old journalist's instincts for a promising story seemed to kick in. "Did you hear about the shooting out in the Big Triangle yesterday?"

"Wait, before you start, let me get us some coffee. I've got a pot brewing in the kitchen and I know how you are about coffee."

"You read my mind." Rivera had wanted coffee since he'd entered the house and his nostrils picked up the aroma.

Carey returned with two mugs full of steaming coffee. He handed one to Rivera and sat down.

"Of course I heard about the shooting, Manny. This is a small town."

Rivera had always suspected Carey got a lot of his information from Millie Ives, the sheriff's dispatcher. She had been a close friend of Carey's wife. That thought caused an idea to flash in Rivera's mind. Millie was a widow— maybe he could find a way to pair the two of them up.

Rivera took a sip of coffee. "Great coffee, thanks. Yeah, I figured your investigative antennae had probably picked up the news."

"I heard one of those militia guys got shot by some bighorn poachers. What do those militia people call themselves? *The Keepers of Order?*"

"Yeah. So much for keeping order. Thus far, all they've accomplished is to get Zeke Stanton shot. He's still in ICU over in Grand Junction."

Carey shook his head. "What do they know about enforcing the law? Or anything else for that matter? That bunch is a few cards short of a full deck. Who got them started on such a nutty idea?"

"A local by the name of Butch Jeffers. You know him?"

"Not personally, but I've heard about him, and from what I understand, he's nothing but trouble. And he's politically connected."

"Right. Anyway, the group consists of four locals, maybe more that I don't know about. I've since learned it's a statewide organization started by a guy from Price who split off from the Western States Freemen to start his own militia. I guess the Freemen weren't radical enough for him."

"What have you learned so far about the shooting?"

Rivera took another sip of coffee and shook his head. "Not a whole lot. It took place in a remote canyon east of the McGinty Ranch. It was a close-up shot. I couldn't find a spent shell, so the bullet was probably fired from a revolver."

"I've driven past McGinty's ranch a couple of times but I've never gone in there," said Carey. "I met him in

Moab once. Salt of the earth kind of guy. Runs cattle on that godforsaken land. He and his wife have lived out there for forty years or more."

Rivera told Carey everything he'd learned from John Singleton about bighorn sheep, then steered the conversation toward the Center for Cosmic Consciousness. "Adam Dunne told me the only human beings who live around there besides the McGintys are the people at the Center for Cosmic Consciousness. Didn't you do a freelance article on that place a while back?"

Carey nodded. "I started a piece because the name of the place sounded so interesting, but I never finished. I was just getting into it when Rita came down with pneumonia, so I dropped it. Let me get my notes."

Carey pushed himself out of his chair with a grunt and padded over to his desk. He sorted through a stack of files, extracted one, and returned to his seat. He put on his reading glasses and paged through the file. "I got as far as visiting the place once and interviewing the director. His name is Timothy Pierce. He's a former Benedictine monk who spent a couple of years at the Monastery of Christ in the Desert. You know that place? It's in New Mexico, way back in a remote canyon on the Chama River. Not far from the Ghost Ranch. He was removed from his job as a parish priest and assigned to the monastery because he'd been hitting the bottle a little too hard. He was pretty open about what had happened. He said some of his parishioners

complained of smelling booze on his breath in the con-
fessional. But that wasn't his only problem. He'd also
developed some serious doubts about his religion. He
told me he'd spent months praying and meditating at
the monastery, trying to reconnect with his faith, but
he never could do it. Finally, he left the priesthood.
Turns out he was heir to some money and 320 acres
of land out in the Big Triangle. The only structure on
the place was an off-the-grid log cabin. He decided to
use his inherited money to turn the place into a retreat
venue for lost souls like himself who were seeking the
meaning of life. He built eight cabins and a central
meeting facility. He brought in a guru by the name
of—let me see—" Carey licked his forefinger, riffled
through the papers in the file, and pulled one out. "Yes,
here it is. Siddhartha Singh. He's from India. He's in
charge of group meetings and individual counseling."

"That's an odd kind of operation to have out in the
Big Triangle. What does the place look like?"

Carey extracted a sheet of paper and some photographs from the file. "Here's a sketch of the layout
of the buildings and a few photographs of the place."
Carey pointed with a pencil at the layout as he spoke.
"You drive through the main gate and the office is up
ahead on the left. It's built onto the front of Pierce's
residence. Next to that is the guru's residence. On
the right is a meeting facility with a small cafeteria.
Beyond that are eight cabins, four on each side of a

gravel driveway. Pierce had a power line run all the way over from McGinty's place. On the north end of the property where some real rocky terrain begins, is the original cabin. Pierce never ran power to it because he wanted it to remain as an off-the-grid escape to be used by anyone desiring such quarters. The eight new cabins and the original cabin are available for rent by those wishing to benefit from the program."

"Why did Pierce name it the Center for Cosmic Consciousness?'

"I asked him that question. He said he chose the name to reflect man's quest to find meaning in the world. He felt the answer resided not in holy books and church precepts but somewhere in the cosmos. I didn't have time to pursue all that with him during my visit. I'd intended to dig into that a lot more on subsequent visits but then, as it turned out, I never went back." Carey looked forlorn for a brief instant, then he smiled. "If you've got some time to kill while you're out there, you might want to pick up on that conversation. I'd be interested in knowing the details of why a priest gave up on his religion."

Rivera nodded. "I'd be interested too—I'll see if he's willing to talk about it."

"I didn't meet any of the residents but I understand you can stay as long as you wish. That is, if you can afford it."

"How much does he charge?'

"I never got into specifics with him, but judging by the quality of the facilities, I'll bet it isn't cheap."

"Did you meet the guru?"

"Just briefly. A small, brown-skinned man with a soft voice and round rimless glasses. He shaves his head and wears a white robe. He'll remind you of Mahatma Gandhi."

Rivera looked at his watch. "I'd better get going, Chris. It'll take me over an hour to get out there. Anything you can learn about bighorn poaching, McGinty, the folks at the Center, or *The Keepers of Order*, I'd be real interested in hearing about it."

"Sure thing, Manny. I'll get right to work." He smiled. "And thanks for stopping by."

Rivera drove to Wendy's to grab a quick lunch before making the drive to the McGinty Ranch. He'd noticed lately that his waist had expanded from 32 to 33 inches, and that he'd started using the next notch on his belt for a more relaxed fit. Gloria loved salads, ate them often, and encouraged Rivera to do likewise. He knew that was the sensible thing to do. He hopped out of his vehicle intending to order one of Wendy's fancy salads, but when he opened the door and his nostrils got a whiff of hamburgers cooking on the grill, he began salivating and decided instead to order his usual cheeseburger and fries. He justified this quick change of plans with precise logic. There were no restaurants in the barren expanse of the Big Triangle, so it made more sense to eat a solid meal while he had the chance. Eating right could wait until tomorrow.

After lunch, it was time to begin the long drive to the McGinty Ranch. He'd called ahead and spoken to McGinty, making an appointment to visit him. He hadn't disclosed the purpose of the visit, mentioning only that he wanted to ask McGinty a few general questions about the area. No one had answered the phone at the Center for Cosmic Consciousness, so he decided to just drive into the place and take his chances.

After topping off his gas tank, he drove north out of town, turned right, and followed Hwy 128 alongside the Colorado River. He began thinking about Chris Carey and how his life had taken a long slide over the past several years. Once a happily married man, a respected and popular investigative journalist, and an important person in the community, now he was lonely, bored, and well into the downslope of life. To Rivera, it seemed sad that Carey's life was winding down this way, coursing toward the inevitable finish without any chance of reprieve. Rivera wondered if that's what happened to everyone. Decided it probably did. That started him reflecting on his own life.

His relationship with Amy Rousseau had ended rather abruptly last year. She was a beautiful 26-year old with hair the color of honey. She was funny, smart, and full of life. A PhD in plant biology, she had spent a year at the Dolores River Research Institute on sabbatical.

They'd met in connection with one of his cases and saw each other on a regular basis after that. They'd grown close, but it turned out her professional career was far more important to her than Rivera had originally judged. It was only when she told him she was leaving Moab for an opportunity to become an assistant professor at the University of Hawaii that he realized he was a distant second in importance to her career. During that discussion, she'd also revealed that she didn't want children, so he'd been doubly disappointed. He was unhappy at the time but eventually he'd accepted the idea that a life with Amy wasn't meant to be.

They'd had fun while it lasted. Then, earlier this year, Rivera met Gloria Valdez while he was in Rio Arriba County, New Mexico, investigating a cold murder case. She was a deputy sheriff there, divorced from an abusive husband and without children. She was a classic Hispanic beauty in her early thirties with a striking face, long dark hair, and a stunning figure. She'd made no secret of her interest in Rivera, but he had just gotten the news about Amy's plans to leave for Hawaii and wasn't in the right frame of mind to begin a new relationship. He'd left New Mexico immediately after breaking the case he was working on. Although he'd found Gloria attractive, his thoughts at that time had centered on Amy.

While in New Mexico, he'd promised the murdered victim's mother he would return from Utah with her son's remains and bring her the young man's personal journal. By the time he'd returned to New Mexico to fulfill his promise, he'd accepted Amy's departure and the fire he felt for her had dissipated. He reconnected with Gloria at the murdered son's reburial and they'd been seeing each other a couple of times a month ever since, each visit bringing them closer.

Rivera turned off the pavement just before the Dewey Bridge and continued on the gravel road toward the Dolores River. The road transitioned to dirt and, after two miles of dodging ruts, potholes, and rocks, he arrived at the river. It seemed to be running stronger than yesterday. He stopped, slid out of his vehicle, studied the flow, and judged that with some luck he'd be able to make it across. He hoisted himself back into his pickup, drove to the edge of the river, and shifted into four-wheel drive. He let the pickup roll slowly down the bank, the vehicle rocking back and forth as it descended. He felt a sense of relief as the front wheels made contact with the gravel bar. He removed his foot from the brake pedal and gingerly stepped on the gas. Wavelets lapped against the right side of his vehicle. The pickup advanced slowly, the sound of crunching gravel reassuring Rivera he was traversing the river in the right place. He gripped the steering wheel tightly, hoping a front wheel wouldn't find a hole in the gravel and sink to its axle. Twenty seconds later, he was across the river without incident. He exhaled audibly as he gunned the engine and climbed the bank on the far side.

He continued on the dirt road just as he'd done yesterday and ascended the switchbacks to the top of Hotel Mesa, noticing something his mind hadn't tuned into yesterday because he'd been preoccupied with rushing to the scene of the shooting. The long blades of grass on the mesa, now golden from the cold nights, were bending in billowy waves as the massaging of the gentle breeze caused the stalks to ebb and flow in unison. The sea of grass was interspersed with dark green junipers. Yellow snakeweed and clusters of purple wildflowers bloomed along the side of the road. Rivera considered beholding beautiful scenes like this to be one of the perks of his job.

Soon he was headed north where BLM Route 109 transitioned to BLM Route 107. He drove through the hilly terrain with the window open, enjoying the cool air and the peacefulness of the high desert. The sky was deep blue and populated with bright white, puffy cumulus clouds. Two ravens circled in the distance, riding a thermal to higher altitudes. He wondered where they were headed.

Rivera was hoping this journey would not be in vain. He needed to find a starting point—a fact or an event that would launch his investigation on a sensible trajectory. Perhaps a name or a vehicle description or maybe even a license plate number—something tangible to grab onto. Without that, he doubted he would make any headway in identifying the poachers.

# 4

AT ONE THIRTY, Rivera arrived at the McGinty Ranch. The entrance was plain, nothing about it suggesting an ego that needed to impress. The barbed wire fence on each side of the entry road ended at a cattle guard, and a hand-painted sign with the name *McGinty* was nailed to one of the fence posts. Rivera had seen all types of ranch entrances, some with a high, curving stone wall on each side of the entry road, an electric-powered, wrought iron gate, and the name of the owner in bronze letters on the gate. There was no purpose for these elaborate entryways other than to satisfy a man's need to boast of his riches. To Rivera, they projected a message that said *I'm more important than you are. Keep out.* The entrance to McGinty's place said, *This is a working man's ranch; you are welcome to visit.*

Rivera's pickup rattled across the cattle guard and onto the ranch. The rutted dirt road wound its way west across sage flats and around rocky outcroppings. Rivera knew this land of sparse vegetation and infrequent rainfall couldn't support much grazing, so he wasn't surprised to see only a few head of cattle grazing in the fields. After a couple of miles of mostly downslope driving, Rivera saw a ranch house, a barn, and several outbuildings in the distance. The house was constructed of debarked timbers and sat on the edge of a grassy knoll that sloped down to the Colorado River. The river was reddish brown and its banks were green with thick tamarisk. An older man was standing in front of the house watching Rivera approach.

Rivera got out of his vehicle and the man walked over to him. He had a slight limp.

"I'm Alvin McGinty." He extended his hand. "You must be Deputy Rivera."

Rivera shook his hand. "Thanks for seeing me." McGinty was a short, stocky man with the kind of blotchy skin typical of those who spend their lives working outdoors under the high-altitude sun. He looked to be well into his seventies, but his handshake was strong and firm. He was looking up at Rivera with a curious expression, his pale blue, watery eyes locked onto Rivera's as though intent on measuring what kind of man this visitor was. Staring this way at a new acquaintance wasn't a practice one would expect to encounter in a city or even a small town like Moab. Rivera figured it was a result of living in a remote area all your life and rarely seeing other human beings. One had to carefully size up each newcomer.

Rivera scanned the view from the house down to the river. "This is a beautiful place you've got here."

"Yeah. It's a hidden gem. Most river frontage is a high canyon wall that drops straight down to the river, but here the river made a slow, wide bend that left a gently sloping bank on this side."

Rivera noticed a dozen or more head of cattle grazing halfway down the slope near a trio of cottonwood trees. Then he looked closer. There was what appeared to be a mule deer right in the middle of the herd. "Is that a deer grazing with the cattle?"

McGinty turned, shaded his eyes with his hand, and smiled. "Yeah. It's the damnest thing. That mule deer is always out there with the cattle. She thinks she's a cow. The wife and I call her Marybell."

"That's a first for me," said Rivera, shaking his head. He pulled a notepad and pen from his shirt pocket. "Mr. McGinty, I wonder if you're aware that there's been some bighorn sheep poaching going on in this general area."

McGinty looked surprised. "Am I aware? Of course I'm aware. I love those bighorn sheep. Junie, that's my wife, she calls them majestic. She says they have a look of intelligence in their eyes. And I believe she's right. There's a bunch of them out in that rocky country east of here. I've seen them poachers out here several times. The first time I called your sheriff about it was nine months ago."

"Oh. I didn't know you'd called." Rivera suddenly felt defensive. "What did the sheriff say?"

"Frankly, he didn't seem very interested in what I was telling him. He sure didn't send anyone to arrest them."

"What was it you saw?"

"I was returning from visiting a friend in Glade Park. I saw three men coming out of the rocks. One had a rifle. The other two were carrying the decapitated head of a bighorn—one guy grasping each horn. They put it under a tarp in the bed of a gray Ford pickup just as I was approaching. I figured they were bad hombres so I pretended not to notice what they were doing as I drove by. Just gave them a wave and continued on. When I got home, I called the sheriff."

"Did you tell him about the bighorn head?'

"Sure. He asked me if I was positive that's what it was. I said yes. He sounded doubtful. He asked me if I'd gotten the license plate number. I said no, but told him it was a gray Ford pickup with Colorado plates. He said there were a lot of gray Ford pickups in Colorado. He asked me if I recognized any of the men. I said no. He seemed to be in a hurry. He thanked me and hung up. That was pretty much how the conversation went."

Rivera was shocked. "And that was it?"

"Yeah, until the next time I saw them. That was about four months ago. I was out on the northeast corner of my place—out where that real rocky terrain begins—fixing some fencing."

"What did you do?"

"Well, I wasn't going to call the sheriff again. I knew that would be pointless. So I did something stupid. I got my rifle out the truck and fired a warning shot. Hit a rock about ten feet from them. I'm a good shot so I knew there was no way I'd accidentally hit one of them. Those sons o' bucks started firing back. I believe they intended to hit me. And damn near did. I dove for cover behind a rock. They fired at least a dozen rounds at me. One of them bullets put a hole in the door of my pickup. I waited awhile after the shooting stopped and then got out of there. It was a dumb thing to do. It's just me and the missus living alone out here."

Rivera jotted notes into his notepad. "Did you report the incident?"

"Yeah, after they fired at me, I thought I'd better report it. I called that sheriff of yours again. He listened to my story and then blamed me—said I had no business firing at them. I told him those were the same guys I'd called him about before—the ones who were poaching the bighorns. Didn't he mention this to his deputies?"

Rivera shook his head. He was ashamed and embarrassed. Sheriff Campbell hadn't mentioned it to the staff at all. Rivera felt a familiar resentment rising within him. Campbell had done things like this before.

He was not only incompetent—he was lazy and derelict in his duties. McGinty's calls had probably arrived around Campbell's tee time.

"Have you seen those men since?"

"Several times. Now whenever I see them, I call Butch Jeffers in Moab. He has a group that's trying to get rid of those lawbreakers. I forget what they call themselves."

"Is it *The Keepers of Order*?"

"Yeah, that's it. I heard about them a while back when I was in Moab picking up some fencing supplies. If the Sheriff's Office won't do anything about them poachers, then maybe Butch can get the job done."

"What do you mean by *get the job done*?"

McGinty hesitated. "You know, scare them off or arrest them or something."

It was the *or something* that worried Rivera. "How do you know the guys you saw were the poachers?"

"I studied them with my binoculars. There's no doubt in my mind. It was the same three guys I saw the first time."

"Can you describe them?"

"Mid-twenties or thirties, Anglo, one tall with a dark beard, the other two medium height."

"What about hair color?"

"They were wearing hats."

"When was the last time you saw them?"

"I saw them yesterday morning."

"And then you called Butch Jeffers?"

"That's right."

Rivera put the notepad back into his pocket. "Something bad happened out there yesterday. A young man named Zeke Stanton was shot and seriously wounded." McGinty's eyebrows rose. "He was one of the militia people with Jeffers who went looking for the poachers. So you'd better be real careful if you see the poachers again. They're dangerous people. And make no mistake, there's a lot of money to be made poaching bighorns, so this isn't just a bunch of yahoos trying to make a quick buck. They're well organized and well equipped."

"Damn. How's the Stanton boy doing?"

"He's still in ICU."

McGinty looked at the ground and shook his head. "I kind of feel responsible—"

"It's not your fault. You did what you thought was right." In Rivera's mind, it was Denny Campbell who was responsible. Rivera handed McGinty one of his cards. "Call me if you see them again. And stop calling Jeffers. Leave law enforcement to the professionals."

"Sure thing, Deputy. And be careful if you go out into that rocky country where the bighorns are. You're a sitting duck for a rifle shot out there."

Rivera drove off the McGinty Ranch, crossed the cattle guard, and continued on BLM Route 107 which now made a ninety degree turn and headed east. A quarter mile later, he spotted James Kirtland crossing the road. Like yesterday, he was dressed in camouflage clothing and carrying a rifle. Kirtland waited by the side of the road for Rivera.

Rivera rolled to a stop. "You boys at it again?"

Kirtland inhaled and straightened up. "Butch aims to get the job done, Manny. He's our leader and he says we've got to press on no matter what. Until the job's finished."

"Did you get another tip they were here today?"

"No tip today. Butch just figured they might not have gotten a bighorn yesterday because of Zeke being in the way, so maybe they would come back today."

"James, I've known you ever since I came to Moab six years ago. We've played basketball together, as opponents and on the same team. I like you. But have you lost your damn mind? Have you already forgotten what happened to Zeke?"

Kirtland's shoulders slumped slightly. "Yeah, I know, Manny. But my loyalty is to Butch. I took an oath when I joined the militia. And I aim to keep it."

"Butch is going to get you hurt. Or worse. Don't be foolish. This militia thing you joined might be well intentioned, but their methods aren't very smart. And from what I've learned so far, those poachers aren't amateurs. They're well organized and well-armed. You don't have a chance against them. Understand? No chance."

A hint of worry began to intrude on Kirtland's look of bravado. "Just the same, Butch wants us to stay on the job. And by the way, he's not too happy with you. Better be careful around him. He swore that the next time you two tangle, the outcome will be very different."

Rivera shook his head. "James, if you won't turn around and go home, at least be real careful out there. The poachers fired at Mr. McGinty awhile back for intruding on their business. He's lucky to be alive. And Zeke's in ICU." Rivera handed him a business card. "Better to call me if you see something than to try and handle it yourself." He drove off, disgusted with the whole situation. Neither Butch nor James had a whole lot of sense, but Rivera blamed Sheriff Campbell. Things had gotten totally out of hand. Events should never have been allowed to go this far. Rivera was beginning to get a bad feeling about the whole affair.

# 5

RIVERA CONTINUED EAST on BLM Route 107 toward the Center for Cosmic Consciousness, eager to find out more about it. He was curious about the Center and his head was filled with questions. Why was it established? Who were its clients? What kind of people were they? And why did its founder leave the priesthood and choose this new life?

Rivera drove past the dead-end two-track he'd used to access the crime scene yesterday and continued for another half mile to the entrance of the Center for Cosmic Consciousness. The entryway was nothing more than a narrow gravel drive, nondescript and unmarked except for a small sign that read *Private Drive*. None of the Center's buildings could be seen from the road.

He turned left and followed the driveway through a dense stand of junipers into a narrow canyon. The driveway zigzagged through a field of cottonwood trees and large red rock boulders, and continued alongside a small creek which trickled through the canyon. After a quarter mile, the canyon widened and Rivera could see the Center in the distance. It was nestled in a small valley framed by looming red rock cliffs. The buildings were constructed of spruce logs and the layout was just as Chris Carey had described. Rivera's immediate impression was that the Center looked well cared for and expensive, and he wondered again what possessed a man to establish a retreat out here in the middle of nowhere.

He drove up to the first building on his left, parked, and got out of his vehicle. There was a sense of tranquility about the place. The only sounds he heard were the cottonwood leaves rustling in the breeze and the caws of a raven echoing off the canyon walls. He walked to the door marked *Office* and knocked. Thirty seconds later, a man with a shaven head who looked to be in his mid-forties opened the door. He was wearing black trousers and a snug-fitting black T-shirt. He had sharp features with a Roman nose and brown eyes. Tanned and trim, he had the body of a man who ate right and stayed in shape. An expression of nervous worry filled his face.

"Oh, thank God you're here. What took you so long?"

"Took me so long? I don't understand. Were you expecting me?"

"Of course. I called the sheriff early this morning, Deputy...um..." He studied Rivera's nametag. "... Rivera. And I'm Timothy Pierce. At the Center, I'm known as Brother Timothy."

They shook hands. "Nice to meet you, Brother Timothy, but why did you call the sheriff?"

"Because of Dr. Peter Kennedy. He's never done this before. Didn't the sheriff tell you?"

Sheriff Campbell hadn't mentioned anything. By now, things like this no longer came as a surprise to Rivera but they still embarrassed and irritated him. No doubt Campbell was too busy campaigning for re-election to bother with the problems of a mere citizen. "What did Dr. Kennedy do?"

"He walked off yesterday and never came back."

"I'm not aware of any of this, Brother Timothy. I came to ask if you knew anything about the bighorn sheep poaching that's been going on around here. Why don't you start from the beginning and tell me exactly what happened?"

Brother Timothy looked distraught, shook his head. "I can't believe the sheriff didn't follow up on my call." He invited Rivera into the office where they sat in straight back chairs at a small table. Through a doorway, Rivera could see a large, well-furnished living room. That it was plush would be an understatement.

"As I told the sheriff earlier, Dr. Kennedy is one of our residents. He's lived here for about two years. Every day, during his free time between counseling sessions, he hikes into the backcountry. This is something we encourage all of our residents to do—wander alone through the canyons and across the mesas, find a comfortable place with a pleasant view, sit down, and use the solitude and silence of the high desert to relax and clear their minds. When Dr. Kennedy taught at the university, his field was anthropology with a specialty in petroglyphs. He dropped out of university life, but petroglyphs are still his passion. Around here, there's an abundance of petroglyphs on the rocks, so he enjoyed spending his alone time searching for new ones. Yesterday morning, like always, he went out into the backcountry by himself with his camera. Sheila Nelson, his longtime girlfriend who lives here with him, informed me late last evening that he never came back. She's worried sick. Can you please help us?"

"I'll do what I can, but people disappear for all kinds of reasons. Sometimes it's by choice." Rivera had the option of calling in the Search and Rescue volunteers, but before he did that, he wanted to learn more about what had happened leading up to the disappearance. Maybe there was a simple explanation. Maybe Dr. Kennedy decided for personal reasons to leave the Center and leave his girlfriend too. Also, with the militia and the poachers possibly facing off in a shootout, he didn't want to put the Search and Rescue volunteers in harm's way without good cause. "Has anyone gone looking for him?"

"No. I was hesitant to tell the other residents he was missing. I was worried it might have a negative effect on their psychic recovery process. He wasn't at lunch or dinner yesterday and he missed breakfast this morning. Meal times at the Center are flexible, so none of the others particularly noticed his absence."

"What about his girlfriend? Did she go looking for him?"

"Sheila's handicapped. She has to support herself with a cane when she walks, so she wouldn't make it very far in the rocky terrain around here."

Rivera found himself in an unexpected situation. Now he had two problems—bighorn poachers willing to shoot people and a missing anthropologist. His immediate thought was that the two problems were related. Same area, same timing. His mentor, former Sheriff Leroy Bradshaw, had taught him never to trust coincidences. *Look for a connection*, he would counsel.

"How about we start by you telling me about the Center and showing me around? After that, I'd like to meet with each of the residents individually. See what they can tell me about Dr. Kennedy."

"Sure," said Pierce. "The building we're in right now serves as the Center's office and also my residence. Let's go outside and I'll give you the grand tour."

They left the office and walked down the gravel driveway which bisected the compound. Pierce pointed to the various buildings as he spoke. "The cabin next to mine is where our resident guru, Brother Siddhartha lives. He's inside now, either meditating or reading. The larger building across the way houses our cafeteria, library, and meeting rooms. We call it the Community Center." To Rivera's ear, Brother Timothy's sentences seemed to be delivered with the cadence of a preacher at the pulpit. "You'll notice as we walk that the environment here is quiet and activity is unrushed. That's the way we want it. Most people come here to find themselves, not to meet new friends, so we encourage solitude except during meals and group sessions. Many of our residents have become psychologically lost and seek to become grounded again. They've reached a point in life's journey where they're questioning the path they've chosen and are now reevaluating it. In most cases, the value system they used to guide their lives was inherently self-defeating—either materials based or self-indulgent or both. Some of our residents are simply searching for the meaning of life. Others have gotten lost just trying to make it through the day-to-day challenges of human existence. Whatever the nature of their problem, our job is to help them heal themselves and find contentment. Contentment is the goal."

"How many residents do you have?" Rivera took out his notepad.

"Besides Dr. Kennedy and Sheila, there are currently five others." Pierce gestured with his arm. "They live in these cabins."

Rivera scanned the cabins. There were eight of them, four on each side of the driveway. They were all identical, about a thousand square feet and rectangular in shape. Each had a small, covered porch in front with a single rocking chair and a side table. Some of the cabins had vehicles parked alongside them. "Where do Dr. Kennedy and Sheila live?"

"There's an old cabin on the back end of the property, about a half mile down that road." He pointed to a two-track that left the compound and headed north. "It's the original ranch house. It's off the grid—no electric power except what's produced from a solar cell array and a small windmill. It has a well and a septic tank. The rest of the complex has electric power, indoor plumbing, and the other modern conveniences our residents expect."

"Who are the other residents?"

"One is a woman by the name of Harriet, an oil painter who's been here for about six months. Another is a photographer named Bob who arrived about a month ago. Then there's Joey, who was a bass player in a seventies rock band." Pierce laughed. "I think they called themselves the Purple Turtles or something like that. Joey's been here over a year. He's got some serious problems to work out, but I'm hopeful. I hate to see anyone leave here without completing their journey to becoming whole. It does happen from time to time, and when it does, I always consider it a personal failure."

"Do these people have last names?'

"We generally just use first names at the Center, but I have their full names in the office files."

"I'll need those and their home addresses."

"Of course. The fourth resident is a poet named Claudia who writes sonnets about the backcountry and the creatures who live there. Lastly is Theodore, a wealthy scion of the newspaper industry who's been here for almost a year. Besides the residents, we have a support staff of three. They live in Glade Park, Colorado, just across the state line. Their names are Homer and Gladys Jones and their daughter's name is April. They commute every day across the Big Triangle. That's everyone."

Pierce told Rivera which resident lived in which cabin, the deputy jotting the information into his notepad.

"I know that Bob and Joey are in their cabins now. So is Sheila. The others are scattered out in the backcountry communing with nature."

That fact alarmed Rivera. "Excuse me a moment." He walked a short distance from Pierce, pulled out his cell phone, and called Alvin McGinty. The rancher answered after four rings.

Rivera spoke in a hushed voice. "It's Deputy Rivera. Any sign of the poachers so far today?"

"Haven't seen a one of 'em yet. I'll keep my eyes open and call you if I do."

"Okay, thanks. It's important. Some people from the Center are wandering around out there in that rocky terrain."

"I understand."

Rivera clicked off and walked back to Pierce. "I'll interview everyone who's here now. Afterwards, I'd like to stop by the office and pick up the full names and addresses of the residents."

"No problem. I'll have a list ready for you."

Rivera left Pierce, walked to cabin number six, and knocked.

Bob, the photographer, pulled open the door. He was holding a book with a worn leather cover, his index finger serving as a bookmark. "Yes sir, can I help you?"

Rivera introduced himself. "I'm investigating the disappearance of Dr. Peter Kennedy and I'd like to ask you a few questions."

Bob's eyebrows rose. "Dr. Kennedy has disappeared? I didn't know. What happened?" Bob was six feet tall with dark eyes and a long, serious face. His brown hair fell to his shoulders and he appeared to be in his late twenties.

"That's what I'm trying to find out. When was the last time you saw him?"

Bob thought for a moment. "Yesterday morning, about eight-thirty I'd guess. I was just finishing breakfast in the cafeteria when Dr. Kennedy and his girlfriend walked in."

"Did he seem upset about anything? Was he his normal self?"

"He didn't seem upset, at least as far as I could tell. I don't know him well enough to tell you if he was his normal self. I've only been here a month. We residents don't spend a lot of time socializing with one another. The idea here is to relax, meditate, and try to find contentment."

Rivera chatted with Bob for a few minutes and learned little except that he lived in a rent house in Spanish Valley south of Moab and aspired to one day become a famous photographer. He'd brought his camera equipment with him to the Center and enjoyed photographing the geologic formations, animals, and sunsets during his backcountry journeys in search of solitude.

Rivera walked across the driveway to cabin number three where Joey, the former rock star lived. He knocked on the door. Joey, a tall, gaunt man wearing jeans and a faded Grateful Dead T-shirt opened the door. He had a three-day stubble, a gray ponytail, and dilated pupils. Rivera guessed his age at sixty. Joey studied Rivera with a wary eye as marijuana smoke wafted out of the cabin.

Rivera introduced himself and explained that he was investigating the disappearance of Dr. Kennedy.

"Kennedy disappeared?" Joey's expression changed from one of wariness to one of delight. He emitted a throaty, smoker's laugh which sounded almost like a cough. "Well, good. I hope the sonofabitch never comes back. I always found him kind of pretentious. A pseudo-intellectual type, you know what I mean? Always talking like he's smarter than everyone else. And he's at least twenty-five years older than that live-in girlfriend of his. I don't like being around him. It messes with my karma, man."

Rivera wasn't concerned about the marijuana. It was legal in Colorado which was only a few miles away across the empty landscape of the Big Triangle. To him, it seemed silly to have it legal on one side of an imaginary line running through the middle of nowhere and illegal on the other side. Rivera believed marijuana was nothing more than a plant that people had been getting high on for thousands of years. It did no real harm. His grandmother used to grow it in her backyard for use in making a salve she rubbed on his grandfather's arthritic joints. Rivera had his own rules about enforcing marijuana laws. He chose not to bust users—they rarely did any harm. Why ruin a kid's life just because he succumbed to teenage peer pressure and tried a joint? But Rivera never hesitated to arrest a dealer. Dealers were known to encourage kids to graduate to stronger, even lethal, drugs like crystal methamphetamines and opioids. Sheriff Campbell, a stickler for enforcing the law, had accused Rivera several times of making up his own laws. He'd even threatened to fire him once. But Rivera's police work was guided by a credo his grandfather had given him early in the deputy's career: *Justice is more important than the letter of the law.* Rivera believed marijuana should be legalized but never mentioned his feelings to anyone. He knew it would be a long time before it was legalized in predominantly Mormon Utah.

Rivera learned from Joey that he too had last seen Dr. Kennedy at breakfast yesterday morning. Kennedy had been lecturing anyone who would listen about how ignorant most people were about petroglyphs and their history. According to Joey, Kennedy had gone on and on about how it wasn't only the Ancient Americans who'd pecked them into the rock faces, but also the Spaniards, the modern-day tribes, and even some early twentieth-century cowboys.

"It was as though Kennedy was lecturing us," Joey said. "The pompous ass was treating us like a bunch of grade school kids. Talking down to us like we were uneducated hicks so fortunate to have such a brilliant man bestowing his wisdom on our inferior minds."

"So you resented him?"

"I came here because I'd had enough of city life and city people, and Kennedy reminds me of the people I've been trying to steer clear of. All the stuff Sid preaches is well and good, but my main reason for being here is solitude."

"Who's Sid?"

"Siddhartha Singh, our guru. I call him Sid for short." Joey laughed. "I don't think he likes that. Anyway, I plan to finish out my years by myself here at the Center."

Rivera learned nothing more of value from the former rock star. He returned to his vehicle, drove to the back of the compound, and located the two-track that led to Kennedy's cabin. As he bumped along the road which gradually sloped upward, the distance between the towering red rock walls on each side of the canyon narrowed. He noticed the terrain becoming thicker with junipers and pinyon pines. The road snaked through the trees and red rock boulders, occasionally crisscrossing the small creek trickling down the center of the canyon. It was a beautiful scene. He stopped his vehicle and opened the window. He inhaled and filled his lungs with the fresh, clean air. The canyon was supremely quiet except for the chirping of a pair of western scrub-jays in the trees. A cottontail rabbit looked up from its lunch of greens and considered the deputy with a motionless stare. Rivera felt fortunate that his job took him to places like this. He smiled, remembering the questions he'd once gotten from city dwellers during a visit to a law enforcement conference in Chicago. *Why do you live in the desert? Isn't it all just a bunch of sand?*

# 6

AS DR. KENNEDY'S CABIN came into view, Rivera wondered what life off the grid was like and what the big attraction was. Just offhand, he couldn't think of many advantages to such an existence. Solitude, maybe. No social pressures. No interruptions. Plenty of time to think about the things one wanted to think about. Still, one could have all that in Brother Timothy's modern cabins. Or a small house in Moab.

Up ahead he saw a weathered, rustic cabin constructed of spruce logs that looked to be over a hundred years old. He rolled to a stop amid a flock of startled chickens. The dwelling was small, about twenty by thirty feet, with a covered porch spanning the front. White smoke rose from a rock chimney and snaked its way into the sky. A solar cell array was situated to the right of the cabin, and a black GMC pickup truck was parked next to it. A small windmill was located in back, its vanes rotating slowly in the breeze and producing a faint, periodic squeak. Behind the cabin, the terrain became rockier and sloped upward toward an array of red rock bluffs and spires.

A young woman with curly, reddish hair and a worried expression sat on the porch steps with her elbows on her knees and her chin resting on her clasped hands. She was small and pretty with a smattering of freckles on her nose. Rivera guessed her age at early to mid-twenties. When she looked up, Rivera could see that her eyes were red as though she'd been crying. She grasped a cane resting on the porch steps and used it to help push herself upright.

"I'm so glad you've come. I'm Sheila Nelson." She hobbled a few steps in Rivera's direction. "I'm so worried. Peter didn't come home last night."

"Yes, I know. Brother Timothy filled me in."

"He left right after breakfast yesterday. He took his camera and his notepad and went into the backcountry, just like he does every morning. But this time he never came back. I think something must have happened to him." She reached out and clutched Rivera's arm. "Could you please find him for me?"

Rivera had seen sudden, unannounced departures before. There could be many reasons for a man's disappearance, especially one leading a lifestyle that was unconventional to say the least. Kennedy was a university faculty dropout living in an off-the-grid cabin with a woman half his age. Normally Rivera wouldn't be overly concerned, but because of the Stanton shooting, he couldn't dismiss the disappearance as simply a free spirit heading off to his next adventure. "I'll do whatever I can, but it would help if I knew more about him."

"I can tell you all about him. Won't you come inside and sit down?"

They entered the cabin and sat facing each other in a small living room, Rivera in a well-worn stuffed chair and Sheila in a matching loveseat. The cabin was warm and a faint scent of pine permeated the air. Logs in the fireplace popped intermittently, showering sparks onto a rock hearth. The furnishings were inexpensive but the room had warmth and character. Rivera saw a small kitchen off to his left and judged that there was a bedroom in the rear. The walls were covered with framed photographs of backcountry scenes, petroglyphs, and indigenous animals. He noticed that two of the photos were dramatic shots of bighorn rams standing majestically high up in the rocks.

"How long has Dr. Kennedy lived here?"

"Almost two years. We came here together after he left the University of New Mexico. He was an associate professor in the Anthropology Department."

Rivera extracted his pen and notepad from his shirt pocket. "Why did he leave the university?"

She sat back and shifted in her seat as if composing her thoughts. "Well, it's kind of a long, sad story, but I'll give you the short version. Peter loved the university environment and was working hard to become a full professor with tenure, but it seemed several of the other professors including his department head thought his research wasn't of sufficiently high quality. He'd published over sixty papers in peer-reviewed journals and given technical presentations at numerous technical conferences. The problem was that much of the anthropology community didn't agree with his theories."

Rivera found himself becoming interested in Kennedy's professional history. He'd heard about this kind of academic warfare while he was dating Amy Rousseau. She'd explained that academia was a brutally competitive arena littered with the hopes and dreams of those who didn't measure up. The notion of professors debating arcane theories on obscure topics in an effort to reach the truth had always appealed to Rivera's curiosity and his interest in logic. To him, the scientific pursuit of new knowledge had many similarities to detective work.

"So what happened?"

"Peter had proposed a theory about a particular type of petroglyph which he'd found in Colorado and Utah. It was a type of shaman figure that he'd discovered in several different locations. After much study and measurements and carbon dating, he put forth the idea that they were early Ute petroglyphs from the late seventeen hundreds and that they were all inscribed by the same man. Peter believed he could track the man's movements by following the petroglyphs he left on the rocks. Many in the anthropology community not only rejected his theory, they branded the conclusions as unimportant and trivial. Peter disagreed. He fought with them on the intellectual battlefield for a long time, but they persisted in rejecting his ideas. After a while, their attacks became more personal than academic. He finally gave up and resigned, dismissing his critics as a bunch of fools. He decided to pursue his interests his own way. Anyway, that's when we came here."

"Did you two meet at the university?'

"Yes. I was a student in a couple of his classes. He's twenty-five years older than I am but there was an attraction between us. When he left the university—I had just graduated—he asked me to come with him. And I did."

"So he's retired? How old is he?"

"He's forty-eight. But he's not really retired. I mean, not in the sense of receiving a pension check every month."

Rivera considered that. "What's his source of income, then?"

"I don't really know, but he always seems to have plenty of money."

A thought crossed Rivera's mind. Was it possible that spotting bighorn sheep for the poachers was Kennedy's source of income? He rejected the idea as soon as he thought of it. Such an activity didn't seem consistent with the interests of an accomplished anthropologist.

"So yesterday morning he went off looking for more petroglyphs?"

She nodded. "That's right. It was part of his daily ritual—something he did rain or shine."

"Did he ever mention a man by the name of Zeke Stanton?"

"Not that I recall."

"What about a militia called *The Keepers of Order*?"

"No. I would have remembered that."

"Does he own a gun?"

"Yes. A pistol. Why are you asking me about his gun?"

Rivera ignored the question. "Did he take it with him yesterday?"

"I don't think so. It should be in the desk."

"Can I take a look at it?"

She shrugged. "I don't see why not." She pointed to the desk. "It's in the top drawer."

Rivera pulled the drawer open and removed a Smith and Wesson .38 caliber revolver. He flipped open the cylinder and sniffed the mechanism. The gun hadn't been fired in a long time. He placed it back in the drawer. "What was Dr. Kennedy wearing when he left yesterday?"

"Tan shirt, tan hiking pants, and his hiking boots." She produced a wan smile. "He was also wearing that silly pith helmet he loves so much. He never went into the backcountry without it. He took a daypack with food, water, his notebook, and his camera gear."

"What about a cell phone? Did he have one with him?"

"No. He didn't own one. He wanted to live a life devoid of modern gadgets. That's why we live out here off the grid."

"Is there anything else you can tell me that might help me find him?"

She thought for a long moment. "No, I can't think of anything else." She frowned and shook her head. "The timing of this is awful. Peter told me one of his former graduate students is coming here for a visit tomorrow. He's a young man who wants to pursue his doctorate specializing in petroglyphs. Peter has been mentoring him for several years."

"What's his name?"

She shrugged. "Harry something. If Peter ever told me his last name, I can't recall it."

Rivera stood up and handed her one of his business cards. "Do you have a way to call me if Dr. Kennedy shows up?"

"There's a phone in the office I can use. If Peter returns, I'll be sure to let you know." She struggled to her feet. "Please find him for me. I'm worried there's something wrong. Maybe he's injured out there. Peter was always so reliable, so predictable. It's not like him to just disappear."

Rivera left the cabin and drove back to the office. Brother Timothy was waiting for him.

"I've made you a list of the residents and the staff members. Full names and addresses." He handed Rivera a sheet of paper.

"Thanks, Brother Timothy. Are the staff members here today? I'd like to talk to them too."

"Yes, they are. Gladys and her daughter April are working in the kitchen at the Community Center, preparing this evening's meals. I think Homer is behind the building doing something to our pickup."

Rivera left Pierce and walked to the Community Center. He entered and passed through the cafeteria, noting the fine furnishings, the expensive Navajo Rugs, the soft piped-in flute music, and the large oil paintings on the walls. The paintings depicted high desert landscapes, beautiful sunsets, and pleasing Zen gardens. All seemed to have been selected for their relaxation-inducing subject matter. He pushed open a pair of swinging doors and entered a spotless kitchen with first-class, stainless-steel appliances and a wall of shiny pots and pans hanging on hooks. It was clear Pierce had spared no expense in the design and construction of the Center for Cosmic Consciousness.

Rivera introduced himself and spoke with Gladys Jones, a mid-forties attractive brunette with large brown eyes. She was wearing jeans and a flowery blouse.

"If you have a minute, I'd like to ask you a few questions about Dr. Kennedy."

"Oh, yes. Brother Timothy just told me he's gone missing." She spoke with a slight lisp. "He had breakfast here yesterday just like he always did. Yesterday was sausage and egg day. We get our fresh eggs from Dr. Kennedy's hens."

"Did you notice anything unusual about his behavior?"

She thought for a long moment. Shook her head. "No, he was his normal self. Talkative and energetic. I didn't notice anything unusual." She turned to her daughter. "April, honey, did you notice anything unusual about Dr. Kennedy at breakfast yesterday?"

April, a teenager with long, straight blonde hair and a snake tattoo the length of her left arm, bit her fingernail in thought. "Nope. I'd say he was just like he always was. Loud and obnoxious."

"April! Don't talk about the residents that way," said Gladys in a chiding tone. "We can't afford to lose our jobs." She looked at Rivera. "I'm sorry, Deputy."

Rivera smiled. "That's okay. No problem."

Rivera thanked them and left the building, searching for Homer. Because Kennedy's demeanor that morning had apparently been consistent with that of previous mornings, Rivera began to worry that maybe Kennedy's disappearance had not been a pre-planned decision. Most men who leave home without an explanation display a behavioral change prior to their departure. The probability that Kennedy's disappearance wasn't voluntary had just ratcheted up a notch. The man could be injured somewhere out in the backcountry. Or worse.

Rivera found Homer behind the Community Center. The hood of a late model, tan, extended-cab Silverado pickup truck was raised, and Homer was leaning inside pouring a can of oil into the crankcase filler tube.

"Howdy," said Rivera.

Homer Jones extracted himself from under the hood and looked at Rivera with surprise and a hint of fear. Rivera had seen that look on people's faces before and it never failed to amuse him. He could always spot the ones with guilty consciences. Their faces displayed a brief instant of earnest concentration during which they engaged in an urgent inventory of their circumstances, trying frantically to decide if they'd just been caught holding incriminating evidence. Since Homer lived in Glade Park, maybe he was the one who transported marijuana from Colorado to the Center. He was probably trying to remember if he had any joints in his pocket.

"Howdy," he said, looking at his hands as he wiped them with an oily rag.

Rivera asked him the same questions about Kennedy that he'd asked everyone else and got the same answers. Nothing had seemed unusual in Kennedy's demeanor or behavior the morning of his disappearance.

A new thought occurred to Rivera. "Did you happen to hear any gunshots yesterday or today?"

Homer raised his eyebrows. "I heard a couple of shots yesterday."

"Could you tell what direction they came from?"

Homer scanned the horizon. Shook his head. "Hard to be sure in this rocky country. Sound bounces off the cliff faces. But if I had to guess, I'd say they came from north or northwest of here."

Rivera considered that. A line north or northwest from the Center would roughly intersect the place where Zeke Stanton had been shot. "Were there two gunshots in quick succession, or were they separated in time?"

"One shot, then several minutes later, a second shot. I figured it was just hunters."

"What time of day did you hear them?"

"I'm not sure. It was somewhere around noon, give or take a couple of hours. I wasn't paying much attention to the time. Hearing gunshots in the Big Triangle isn't unusual."

Rivera jotted the information into his notepad. "Okay, thanks for the information." He started to leave, then stopped.

"Have you ever seen anyone poaching bighorn sheep around here?"

Homer seemed puzzled by the question. "Bighorn sheep? No. I never have. I've seen deer hunters but no one hunting the bighorns."

"Ever heard anyone talk about it?"

Homer shook his head. "No, never have."

Rivera wondered if Homer was being entirely forthcoming. Surely the people living in the tiny hamlet of Glade Park would be aware of the problem. Rivera returned to the office, told Brother Timothy he would get back in touch with him, and drove off. He decided that if Kennedy still hasn't returned by tomorrow, he would notify Search and Rescue and request that they initiate a search. Perhaps he could enlist the assistance of *The Keepers of Order* in the search. If they insisted on being out here, they might as well be doing something useful.

On the drive back to Moab, Rivera called Chris Carey. He brought him up to date on what he'd learned at the McGinty place and the Center for Cosmic Consciousness, and related what Sheila had told him about Dr. Kennedy. He asked Carey to see what additional information he could find out about Kennedy's professional life.

"Anything you can learn about him would be helpful," said Rivera.

"I'll get right on it, Manny." There was a note of enthusiasm in Carey's voice.

Rivera clicked off. He realized there wasn't a whole lot he could do about the poachers until they reappeared, and he would have to depend on McGinty for that information. While he waited for them to return, he would learn more about the black market for bighorns and attempt to attack the problem from the buyers' end. Perhaps he could find a way to backtrack from the hunting ranches to the poachers.

Meanwhile, he would concentrate on the missing Dr. Kennedy. Rivera had a bad feeling there was more to the story than an anthropologist running away from home or lying injured in the backcountry. The coincidence of time and place with the Stanton shooting was worrisome.

# 7

RIVERA SAT IN his office, his attention fixed on the screen of his computer monitor. He'd been checking Alvin McGinty and everyone at the Center for Cosmic Consciousness for wants and warrants. Rivera smiled when he ran Homer Jones's name through the system. He'd been arrested twice for possession of marijuana back in the days when weed was illegal in Colorado. No wonder he'd seemed alarmed when Rivera showed up unexpectedly. Homer probably had some joints in his pocket while standing on Utah soil. No doubt he was the supplier for Joey and anyone else at the Center who wanted the stuff. Other than that, everyone he'd checked had a clean record.

Rivera had also received the ballistics reports on the rifles and handguns he'd confiscated from the militia members. As expected, there was no match for the bullet removed from Zeke Stanton's chest.

Rivera heard his office door open. There was no knock so it had to be Sheriff Campbell. Campbell usually threw the door open so it would slam against the wall and entered with loud bluster. But today his entrance was subdued and polite.

He closed the door quietly and sat down in a visitor's chair. He had a nervous smile on his face and a solicitous manner. "How's it going today, Manny?"

Rivera was surprised and suspicious. Campbell had always referred to him as *Rivera*. And the name was usually uttered with overtones of disdain. This was the first time Campbell had called him *Manny*.

"Just fine, Sheriff."

"Listen Manny, you know the election takes place on Tuesday."

"Sure."

Campbell forced a humorless chuckle. "Well, it turns out the old Army broad I'm running against is a little more popular than I'd given her credit for."

Rivera said nothing but knew where this conversation was headed. Campbell wanted Rivera's help in his campaign for reelection.

"Anyway, I could use all the help I can get."

Rivera smiled and produced an innocent expression that suggested he didn't understand why Campbell was telling him this. He said nothing.

Campbell shifted in his chair. "I know you and I haven't always gotten along real well, but I've always considered you to be my best deputy. Hell, you're the only one in the department who knows anything about conducting an investigation. So I'm asking you to help me out. You're popular and well-liked in the community. If you went out and did a little campaigning for me, I think it would make a big difference in the vote tally."

Rivera had to gird himself to keep from laughing. He played along. "But Sheriff, I've got my hands full with my case load. Poachers are shooting people out in the Big Triangle and now I've learned that an anthropologist living out there is missing." Rivera hated himself for resorting to such passive aggressive foolishness, but he couldn't help himself. Campbell had been a disrespectful, discourteous, incompetent buffoon since the day he took office. And Rivera had been on the receiving end of Campbell's vitriol more than anyone.

"Oh hell, Manny, the shooting was probably just a hunting accident and that anthropologist will show up in a couple of days. I'll bet he's off on a bender or out somewhere with a woman. You can slow your investigation down a little to make some time for helping me out."

"I think there's a fair chance there's going be more trouble out there. I'm hoping I can prevent it."

Campbell's smile was slowly disappearing and a sheen of perspiration was appearing on his forehead. His face was beginning to turn red. "I'm not asking for a lot here. Just two or three hours a day for the next few days."

"Sheriff, I think it would be unethical for me to get involved in the campaign. And campaigning while the county is paying me is probably illegal."

Campbell forced a thin smile. "Nobody's going to care about that. I'll see to it."

Rivera sensed the time had come to wrap up this ridiculous conversation. "If I campaign for you and then you lose, I won't be very popular with the new sheriff. I just can't do it."

Campbell stood up. The metamorphosis in his facial expression was now complete, the solicitous smile reverting back to an angry frown. "Yeah, well don't forget," he bellowed, "if I win, you won't be too popular with me." He stomped out of the office and slammed the door.

Rivera sat back and hoisted his feet onto his desk. He clasped his hands behind his head. He was simultaneously satisfied with his performance and ashamed of his childish behavior. Campbell had a way of bringing out the worst in him. Oh well, he thought, Campbell will get over it. He'll be back on the golf course in no time.

Rivera's telephone rang. It was Chris Carey.

"Manny, I just spoke with an old acquaintance at the University of New Mexico. I helped his daughter get an internship at the newspaper years ago so he owes me one. He's a professor in the anthropology department. He knew all about Peter Kennedy and what had happened with his career. Have you got time for a long story?"

Rivera was hungry. He looked at his watch. "It's getting late in the day. How about we meet at Pasta Jay's for dinner? My treat."

"That sounds great. It'll feel good to get out of the house and have a meal with someone."

"Six o'clock sound okay?"

"That's fine. See you there."

Rivera could feel his body relaxing after the first few sips of Chianti. He was sitting at a table on the outdoor patio of Pasta Jay's restaurant, waiting for Carey to arrive. It was a mild evening, warm for early November. The restaurant was one of Rivera's favorite places, right in the middle of Moab at the corner of Main and Center Streets. He enjoyed relaxing there, watching the people and vehicles pass by.

The traffic light turned green and an orange eighteen-wheeler began moving, its diesel engine growling as it pulled away. It was followed by a dark green Jeep Wrangler with a jacked-up suspension. Next was an old, red flatbed pickup truck carrying hay bales and pulling a horse trailer. Moab was one of the few places between Colorado and Arizona where a person could drive across the Colorado River. It was as though the whole world funneled down to this one place and then opened up again on the other side of the river. For the most part, the river had steep cliffs on one or both sides of it, making road building across the river an expensive proposition. But at Moab, the terrain was low on both sides of the river. That was why the Old Spanish Trail crossed the river here and why U.S. 191 followed the same route today.

There had been a noticeable increase in traffic and tourism during Rivera's six years in Moab. A couple of traffic lights had been added on Main Street during that time and several motels and condo complexes had been built. Moab had been discovered by the outside world and its transformation from a former uranium mining town to an outdoor recreation mecca had taken place. Now, some of the locals who had once wanted more businesses and more jobs to come to Moab were beginning to regret what had happened to their quiet little town.

Despite the increase in traffic density, Rivera still loved the place. He was happy he'd left his hometown of Las Cruces, New Mexico, and moved to Moab. It was the colorful sandstone shapes carved by wind and water over geologic time, the vast empty landscape, the immense views toward the horizon, and the world class sunrises and sunsets that had attracted him to the land of red rock canyons. He'd first seen it as a teenager while on a high school bus trip to Arches National Park. As soon as the opportunity had presented itself, Rivera resigned from his job as a Las

Cruces city cop and accepted a job as a Grand County Deputy.

He remembered when Sheriff Leroy Bradshaw had first hired him. Bradshaw mentored the young, green deputy and nurtured him along, teaching him the proper way to conduct an investigation. He patiently talked to Rivera for hours about how to acquire facts, apply logic, understand people's motivations, and make sensible inferences in order to break a case. He taught him to pay as much attention to what didn't happen as to what did happen, and to establish a precise chronology of events leading up to the crime. Rivera loved working as an investigator. He felt intellectually comfortable with it, as though his mind had been wired for problem solving. A couple of years ago, when Bradshaw left Moab, Campbell entered the picture. Campbell's arrival had diminished Rivera's enjoyment of his work, but, for the most part, Rivera had been able to avoid too much contact with his new boss. Campbell rarely showed any interest in Rivera's investigations and Rivera rarely visited the golf course.

Rivera spotted Carey crossing Main Street. He was walking with a purposeful stride and carrying a manila folder. He was clean shaven and wearing chinos and a yellow, long-sleeve shirt. There was a look of determination on his face, as though he were on an important mission. Rivera smiled. The old investigative journalist was back in the saddle.

Carey entered the patio and came to Rivera's table.

"I've got some really good stuff for you," he said as he sat down.

The waiter took Carey's order for a double Macallan single malt and left.

"Peter Kennedy had some wild theories. They're actually damned interesting. Most of the anthropological intelligentsia thought his theories were more conjecture than fact, but Kennedy bet his whole career on them."

*Conjecture*, thought Rivera. The word stabbed him. That's what had been guiding his thinking ever since he'd visited the Center for Cosmic Consciousness. The bighorn poaching was a fact. The missing anthropologist was a fact. But connecting those two facts was pure conjecture. It was nothing more than a hunch, and if he was wrong, his current course of thinking would lead him nowhere. He could only hope he was right.

The waiter brought Carey a tumbler of scotch and a glass of water. Carey grinned and raised his glass in a toast. "Here's to another successful collaboration."

Rivera smiled and raised his glass. "I'll always drink to that, Chris." He took a sip.

Carey put down his drink, opened the manila folder, and extracted several pages of handwritten notes. "Well, the story goes like this. Kennedy was a bright young student at the University of New Mexico, and earned Bachelor's and Master's degrees in anthropology. He continued on with his studies, completing all the coursework for his PhD. Only his dissertation remained to be written and approved. His interest early on was Native American pottery and the interpretation of the decorative designs baked into the pieces by their creators. He was fascinated by the patterns and thought he might infer something about the early Americans from the details of their work. He was sure the academic community hadn't fully considered the meaning of the patterns, and wanted to explore the field in greater depth. He spent a lot of time digging into what was then the accepted body of knowledge of Ancestral Puebloan, Fremont, and Mogollon pottery. He hoped the topic would be approved by his dissertation committee chairman, but the chairman dissuaded him from pursuing the idea, professing the view that there wasn't much room for new theories in pottery design. Besides, although there were plenty of potsherds to be found in the backcountry, a rigorous study would require complete pieces, not fragments. And, unfortunately, most intact pots were scattered around the world in museums, vaults, and collectors' homes, making detailed inspections difficult. The chairman pointed out that working from photographs would be grossly inferior to studying the real thing, and would therefore be unacceptable. Although Kennedy had his heart set on the topic and insisted he could break new ground in the field, it was to no avail. The chairman admired his student's passion but refused to

accept his proposed dissertation topic." Carey looked
up from his notes, as if making sure the deputy was
following all this.

"So what did Kennedy do?"

"He turned his attention to petroglyphs and pictographs. He told his committee chair that there was
plenty of primary source material available to him.
He just needed to explore the backcountry and find
the rock art. The glyphs were still out there where
they were created, not in museums or private collections. And they existed as whole units instead of
fragments. They were waiting to be studied by anyone
willing to search for and find them. He decided to
rule out pictographs and concentrate on petroglyphs
for two reasons. First, there were far more petroglyphs in existence than pictographs, and second, the
petroglyphs were pecked or carved into the rock and
therefore lasted longer. Pictograph images tended
to fade over time because they were painted on the
rock. It was Kennedy's intention to study petroglyphs
and determine their meaning. He estimated that less
than ten percent of them had ever been observed
by humans and far less than one percent had been
professionally analyzed. Where he got those figures,
nobody knows. It was probably just a guess, something my contact said Kennedy was prone to do a
lot of in his work. Anyway, his dissertation topic was
finally approved and he wrote a creditable volume

titled *A Comparative Study of Shaman Petroglyphs in the Intermountain West."*

Carey turned to the second sheet of notes. "After Kennedy received his PhD, he accepted an assistant professorship at the University of New Mexico. He was an enthusiastic teacher and approached his role in the classroom as more of an anthropology coach than just a teacher. His lectures were always animated and fun. He would bring ancient artifacts to the classroom for freewheeling discussions about why and how they were made, and by whom. He would challenge the students to try and fabricate similar items, and organized a crafts competition to make things more interesting. And he would take the students out to anthropological digs in progress so they could learn proper excavation techniques from professionals and develop a healthy respect for the work. The students loved him. He spent his free time in the backcountry locating, photographing, and cataloguing what he'd found. Over the years, he became a leading expert in petroglyphs."

"Interesting. He sounds like a fine teacher." said Rivera.

"It gets a *lot* more interesting." Carey took a sip of scotch and continued. "He published extensively and was considered a rising star in the world of anthropology. Eventually, he was promoted to associate professor. Life was going his way and his next objective was to become a tenured, full professor. He worked hard, presenting papers at conferences and playing an active role in academic societies and associations. He was beginning to get noticed by others in his field, and not in a good way. He seemed to have a knack for stirring up jealousy and resentment in his peers. Then, one day, he put forth a kind of radical idea. He proposed that the Utes had actually descended from the Fremont people because of some similarities in their petroglyphs. Kennedy seemed to be obsessed with the idea and claimed there was a continuous evolution over the centuries from Fremont glyphs to Ute glyphs. The idea was debunked by his fellow anthropologists, who offered strong evidence that the Utes had not descended from the Fremont people. Kennedy's new theory was probably the beginning of his downfall. To make things worse, he believed he had identified a particular Ute who had inscribed petroglyphs in an area of western Colorado and eastern Utah. He claimed he'd discovered a series of petroglyphs that he believed were all made by the same man in the late 1700s. Other researchers began to challenge the idea. It seemed preposterous to the academic community that a petroglyph could be tied back to a specific individual. About that same time, Kennedy began paying an excessive amount of attention to one of his students, a girl named Sheila Nelson. The whisperings started among the faculty and spread to the academic societies. Academicians whose work had been brushed aside by

Kennedy's early publications began to close ranks on him. At the university, competitors for the rare promotions to full professor began to disparage Kennedy's professional and personal reputation. Kennedy fought back against a torrent of opposition. In a period of two years, he'd gone from being a rock star in the world of anthropology to becoming an also-ran academic grappling for elusive tenure. Finally, one day, he resigned and left the university at the end of the semester." Carey looked up at Rivera.

"So his career was in decline when he left. I guess that's when he moved to the Center for Cosmic Consciousness. It sounds like he just took his girlfriend with him and kind of dropped out."

Carey extracted the last sheet of paper from the file with a flourish. "Wait, Manny. Here's the best part. The place where he found those petroglyphs which he claimed were all inscribed by the same Ute was right there in the Big Triangle."

Rivera's eyebrows rose. "That's interesting. So maybe if I knew where those petroglyphs were, that would be a good place to start looking for him."

Carey thought for a moment. "You might find that information in the academic papers Kennedy wrote."

"Yeah. Not a bad idea. There's a young man arriving in Moab today who Kennedy mentored at the university. His first name is Harry—Sheila Nelson didn't know his last name. He was supposed to visit Dr. Kennedy at the Center tomorrow. I got the impression from Sheila that Kennedy and his visitor, who was also interested in petroglyphs, were close professionally and personally. Maybe Harry knows something about that series of petroglyphs and where to find them. Trouble is, I don't have his last name. I'd really like to talk to him."

"I'll call my contact at the university first thing in the morning and see if I can get the name for you."

"Thanks, Chris. You've been a great help. Now what do you say we order some food. My stomach's beginning to growl."

# 8

MANNY RIVERA SEEMED to wake up hungry every morning, no matter how much he'd eaten the night before. He turned off the alarm clock, swung his feet onto the floor, and rubbed his eyes. He sat there for a long moment, then pushed himself upright and looked out the bedroom window. A hint of first light on the eastern horizon outlined the peaks of the LaSal Mountains with an ethereal glow.

Bentley, his chocolate labrador retriever, was at his side, licking his hand and thumping his tail against the floor, urging Rivera into the kitchen where the dog knew his food was stored. Bentley woke up hungry every morning too.

Rivera went to the kitchen and turned on the light. There were other hungry mouths to feed too—the twenty or so fancy guppies inhabiting the aquarium on his kitchen counter top were huddled in the corner of the tank closest to Rivera, circling and wiggling in anticipation of their morning meal.

He dropped a pinch of tropical fish food into the aquarium and watched the fish dart after the tiny morsels. Then he turned his attention to Bentley who was eagerly awaiting his turn to be served. Rivera filled a bowl with dog food and set it out in the backyard along with a bowl of water. Bentley would eat and then be free to run the fence line with the german shepard next door all day long.

Rivera showered, got dressed, and stepped out of the two-bedroom house he rented into the chilly air. His front yard was covered with a fresh deposit of golden cottonwood leaves, and a few more drifted to the ground as he walked to his pickup. He drove to the Rim Rock Diner on Main Street. It was a popular eating place for locals, and each morning he saw many of the regulars there. Breakfast at the Rim Rock had become one of his favorite parts of the day. The place was like a second home to him.

He parked his vehicle in the lot, walked to the front door, and pulled it open. As always, the smell of sizzling bacon and pancakes on the griddle hit his nostrils and made him salivate. The hum of people in conversation punctuated by the sound of utensils clinking against plates was music to his ears. Hung on the walls were framed black-and-white photographs of early Moab during the uranium boom of the 1950s. Rivera slid into his regular corner booth by the window facing Main Street.

Betty, the waitress who had been serving him breakfast ever since he arrived in Moab, came slinking over to his table with a come-hither expression. She had a carafe of coffee in one hand and a mug in the other. She was in her early fifties and had been divorced four or five times. As usual, her bleached-blonde hair was piled high atop her head and she was wearing a too-tight white uniform. The top three buttons of her blouse were open, exposing a generous cleavage. She stood close to Rivera, her hip touching his shoulder, and slowly poured coffee into the mug. She bent over, now facing him, and placed the mug on the table. She smiled her toothy smile, slowly chewing on a wad of gum. She spoke in a sultry voice, her face close to his. "Did you sleep well last night, handsome?"

By now, Rivera was used to Betty's outrageous, daily flirtations. When he'd first arrived in Moab and started coming to the diner for breakfast, he was intimidated and embarrassed by her advances, but as the years passed, he began to accept them and even look forward to them. He knew he'd miss her if she ever decided to leave her job at the Rim Rock. It was a familiar and comfortable ritual that signaled the beginning of a new day. "I slept just fine, Betty. Thanks. How about you?" As soon as he uttered those last three words, he knew it was a mistake.

"I was lonely, Manny. Thought about you all night long. I tossed and turned, wanting you there with me, keeping me warm. Maybe tonight?"

"Thanks Betty, but I'm involved with someone." He took a sip of coffee. "Her name's Gloria and she's coming to visit tomorrow."

Betty stood up straight, her flirtatious manner now becoming one of mock indignation. "I know. She's the one from New Mexico. A deputy like you."

Rivera was surprised. "How did you know?"

She inhaled deeply and let out an exasperated sigh. "How many times do I have to tell you, Manny? We Rim Rock waitresses know everything that's going on in this town. Information gravitates to our little diner like it's a black hole. You want the usual?"

Rivera nodded and smiled. "Please."

Betty left and Rivera looked out the window. The sun, still not yet over the horizon, was backlighting the mountain peaks with a bright orange glow. The sky was clear blue with a few cumulus clouds to the south—the start of another beautiful day in Moab. He extracted his cell phone and called Alvin McGinty. "Any sign of the poachers this morning?"

"Haven't seen any of 'em yet today. I'll call you if I do."

Rivera thanked him and clicked off. Good—there was no urgency with the bighorn poaching matter. Rivera would have more time to concentrate on the missing Dr. Kennedy. Almost immediately, his cell phone buzzed. The caller was Chris Carey.

"Manny, I called the university this morning and got the name of that young fellow who's coming to visit Peter Kennedy. His name is Harry Ward. According to my contact, he was a protégé of Dr. Kennedy's when Ward was enrolled as a graduate student in anthropology. After Kennedy left, Ward dropped out of school. The young man is supposed to be very intelligent." Carey emphasized the word 'very.'

"Great, Chris. Thanks. I'll see if I can locate him." Rivera clicked off just as Betty returned with his breakfast. It was the same thing he ate every morning—sausage patties, eggs over easy, hash browns, and wheat toast. And more coffee. After finishing breakfast, he sat there feeling a little guilty and wondering if he should be eating something healthier for breakfast. Yogurt and fruit and cereal, or something like that. Maybe he'd try ordering it tomorrow.

He took out his cell phone and began calling the local motels. On the sixth call, he learned that Ward was registered at the Ramada Inn. He paid the tab, left the diner, and drove to the Ramada.

At the front desk, Rivera obtained the telephone number for Ward's room and punched it into his cell phone.

"Hello?"

"Harry Ward?"

"Yes. Who's calling?"

Rivera introduced himself and asked Ward if he was here to visit Dr. Peter Kennedy.

"Why yes, I am. I'm leaving in about thirty minutes to visit him at the Center for Cosmic Consciousness. Is there a problem?"

"I'm afraid Dr. Kennedy is missing. He left the Center on foot a couple of mornings ago and never returned. He might be lost somewhere out in the Big Triangle. Or injured. He doesn't own a cell phone so he can't call for help."

"He's probably out in the backcountry searching for petroglyphs. It's his life. Is there any way I can help?"

"I'm trying to learn as much about him as I can. I'd like to visit you and ask a few questions about him. The Big Triangle is huge, so anything you can tell me that might narrow down the search area would be helpful."

"Sure. I had no idea he was missing."

Rivera found the door to Ward's room and knocked. The door opened and Rivera saw a man in his mid-twenties with light blue eyes and shoulder-length, sun-bleached, blond hair. He was well tanned and had a handsome, chiseled face. He wore dark tan shorts and an orange T-shirt that read "Straight Outta Anthropology." There was a look of concern on his face.

"Come in, Deputy. Please have a seat."

Rivera sat in a straight back chair by the desk and Ward sat on the bed. Rivera started by bringing him up to date on what he had learned at the Center. He figured that if Ward was going to be of any help, it would be best if he knew everything. "Have you ever been to the Center?"

"No. This was going to be my first visit. Dr. Kennedy and I are very close but I've been living in Oregon and haven't seen him in a couple of years. We stay in touch by mail. He's like a father to me. I met him at the university when I was working on my Master's degree in anthropology. I became very interested in his petroglyph research and we used to talk for hours about it. After he left the university, I finished up my Master's program. I wanted to go on for a PhD, but I was short on funds, so I went to work for a couple of years in various jobs—construction, waiting tables, working as a locksmith, laying coaxial cable for a cable TV company, installing bushes and trees for a landscaping company—whatever work I could find. There wasn't much demand for someone with a Master's degree in anthropology. Now I've got enough money saved to go back to school. Dr. Kennedy said he had some ideas for my dissertation topic, so I came here to discuss them with him."

"Sheila Nelson, Dr. Kennedy's girlfriend, told me a little about his career. Then I learned more from a friend of mine who had a contact at the university." He told Ward everything he had learned about Kennedy's professional career and asked if there was anything Ward could add to the story.

"Yeah, I can add quite a lot to that. Dr. Kennedy had a theory—a good one—about a series of Ute petroglyphs he'd found while exploring the backcountry near the Utah-Colorado border. He and I spent hours talking about it when we were at the university. There's a place on Piñon Mesa where there's a pile of large sandstone slabs out in the middle of some sagebrush flats. He said they looked like the remains of a collapsed red rock pinnacle or perhaps the result of some kind of lower-level upthrust. He said there's no particular reason backcountry explorers would want to visit it. From a distance, it just looks like a jumble of nondescript rocks—nothing unusual. He said there are sandstone outcroppings and rocky upthrusts all around that area. But he was looking for petroglyphs and the place looked like it had possibilities, so he hiked over to it one day and checked it out. He said he'd found a unique rock art panel on one of the rock faces. It must have been a special place because there were petroglyphs from the Fremont culture that dated back to around 900 A.D. and many others from the modern-day Utes. He also found markings from Spanish conquistadors and early twentieth century cowboys."

Rivera found himself becoming interested in the details. "How could he tell which petroglyphs were from which group?"

"That was his specialty. For him, it was easy. The Fremont petroglyphs could be analyzed by radiocarbon dating the desert varnish that accumulated in the cuts. Typically, the images were of deer, bighorn sheep, dotted lines, spirals, and shaman figures. I'm sure you've seen many petroglyphs, so you know the animals and shamans were rudimentary stick figures. They were either scraped or pecked into the sandstone with a piece of harder rock."

"I had the opportunity to explore Nine Mile Canyon a couple of times. It's full of Fremont petroglyphs."

"The early Ute glyphs were more lifelike than those of the Fremont people, but they were still pretty rudimentary forms of art. Most were inscribed with a metal tool of some sort, but many were cut the old way using a chunk of harder rock. The Ute glyphs also included images of men on horseback. Those were images of the Spaniards as seen through Ute eyes. Dr. Kennedy had done a lot of work trying to build a timeline of how Fremont art had evolved into Ute art—a very controversial subject and one where most scholars disagreed with him. The Spaniards' petroglyphs were easy to recognize because they usually included religious symbols such as a crucifix or an image of the Blessed Mother. And the cowboys' glyphs were self-dated, as they usually left their names or initials and the date they were there. I'm oversimplifying all this, but you get the general idea. The science of dating these things and interpreting them is complicated and often controversial."

"There must have been something special about that rock that made so many different groups want to leave inscriptions there."

"I asked Dr. Kennedy that same question. He said, no, it was just another flat rock. A target of opportunity. When one group saw earlier glyphs, they added their own. He believed it was just the power of suggestion. Sort of like graffiti today. A wall is clean until someone tags it. Then other graffiti artists feel an urge to add their own designs."

"Did he ever talk to you about a series of petroglyphs he'd found that he believed were all inscribed by the same Ute?"

"Yes." Ward hesitated. "I'm surprised you know about that. He told me about it in confidence. He'd found a particular type of shaman image on that rock I was talking about. It had a trapezoidal body with broad shoulders, stick arms and legs, and a head decorated with a headdress and earrings. It was a Ute glyph from the late 1700s. And here's the part that must remain confidential. I'm only telling you this because I want to help you find Dr. Kennedy. This particular shaman petroglyph caught his eye because of an unusual feature—one of the stick arms was at its side and the other was extended straight out to the side of the body. He'd never seen one like that before and wondered what the significance of the extended arm was. Months later, while he was exploring in that same general area, he found another image just like it about a mile away. He compared photographs of the two images and saw that the designs were almost identical. He told me he began musing about whether they'd been inscribed into the rock by the same artist. Then he laughed at himself for such a ridiculous notion. He quit laughing when he found a third one a month later. It was located about three quarters of a mile from where he'd found the second one. The three roughly lined up, leading in a westerly direction from the rock pile. When he compared the three, they were nearly identical in every way. He became more interested as he inspected the cuts with a field microscope. He noticed that the ridges and valleys left by the jagged edge of the metal tool used to inscribe them were practically identical. When he published his findings and put forth his theory that they'd been created by the same man, the scientific community began to debunk his ideas. Even scoff at him. He'd been resented for his success and his meteoric rise in the scientific community, partly because of his accomplishments and partly because he's sort of, well, a talkative guy with a loud voice. It's hard for others to get a word in edgewise. He enjoys dominating the conversation, driving the subject to the things that interest him, and deliberately stirring up controversy and arguments. Plus he doesn't suffer fools gladly." Ward chuckled. "Despite all that, he and I got along real well."

Rivera wondered if he might find Dr. Kennedy somewhere along that line of petroglyphs. "Did he pursue the series of shaman petroglyphs any farther?"

"Sure. He brought a surveying instrument out there and verified that he could see from the first shaman to the second, and from the second to the third. Each was inscribed on a high point in the terrain, so connecting them with a direct line of sight was possible." Ward leaned forward and lowered his voice. "And here's the important part that must remain absolutely confidential. It's the thing he never told the scientific community. The arm of the first shaman was pointing in the direction of the second shaman, and the second shaman's arm was pointing to the third shaman. It was as though Dr. Kennedy's old Ute had laid out a trail that he wanted to remember. Dr. Kennedy said it was easy to get lost out in that vast, desolate, rocky wilderness, so if you're not familiar with it and want to find your way back to a place you've been to before, what better way to mark the trail?"

Rivera smiled. "Interesting."

"It gets better. Dr. Kennedy got curious about the location of the first shaman. He theorized that it had to be a special place to the Fremont people and the early Utes because they had inscribed so many petroglyphs there. He wondered if perhaps it was a sacred site where the old ones went to pay homage to their gods. If it was, there might be some record of it in the Ute oral histories. That sent him off to the Marriott Library at the University of Utah where he spent weeks reviewing old transcripts of interviews with Ute elders. The interviews were conducted by researchers back in the 1940s. They were recorded and later translated from the Ute language into English. The goal of this program, and many others like it, was to record the origin stories, history, family traditions, mythology, religious beliefs, and folklore of the American tribes before the old ones passed away and their stories, which had been passed down verbally from generation to generation, were lost forever. He found two stories that referred to that rock pile. Turns out it was a place where, on the day of the winter solstice, the light of the setting sun would pass through a small slit in the rocks and bisect a spiral petroglyph. It marked the day when the setting sun stopped moving farther south on the horizon and reversed its direction. According to the stories, members of a band of early Utes went there on that day every year, believing that if they saw the shaft of light bisecting the spiral, it would bring them good luck in their hunts during the coming spring and summer."

"Those petroglyphs might be a good place to start looking for Dr. Kennedy. If I could find them, that is."

"Wait, there's more. Dr. Kennedy found a transcript of an old story about a Ute medicine man who was out collecting herbs one day when he spotted in the distance a lone Spaniard on horseback heading in his direction. The Spaniard was wearing armor and carrying a lance and a sword. There had been a lot of bad blood between the Spaniards and the Utes, so they were arch enemies. Many Utes had been killed at the hands of the Spaniards or sold into slavery. The Ute medicine man concealed himself behind some rocks. When the Spaniard arrived at the rocks, he dismounted, sat down for a rest in the shade, and removed his headgear. The Ute picked up a rock the size of a small watermelon, climbed to a place above the Spaniard, and threw the rock down with both hands, striking the soldier on the head and killing him. Here's where the story gets really fascinating. There's a lot of speculation here, mind you, but that's how most theories start out. I brought a file containing copies of Dr. Kennedy's notes. Let me read you the words of the Ute story as it was passed down through the generations." Ward pulled a file out of his briefcase and opened it. He paged through it and extracted a sheet of paper. "I'll just read the pertinent part."

> *"They say the medicine man was called Buckskin Charlie Posey. He believed the horseman carried his power in his saddlebags. To the Utes, the Spaniard's power was bad medicine. After he killed the Spaniard, the medicine man caught the Spaniard's horse. He removed*

*the saddlebags and opened them. Inside, he found the white man's bad medicine.*

*"They say he carried the saddle bags to a place far away from where his people lived, so that they would never again be victimized by this bad medicine. As he walked, he marked his trail so that he could find his way back to the saddlebags if one day he needed the bad medicine to reverse a curse placed on his people. He walked a great distance and hid the white man's evil in a place where no one but him would ever find it."*

Ward looked up at Rivera. "Isn't that interesting?"

"It is. I'm surprised the anthropology community rejected his ideas."

"Well, he didn't tell them about this part. He kept it to himself. Now, are you ready for the best part of the story?"

Rivera smiled. "I'm ready."

"Dr Kennedy determined through his research into the Ute stories that the Spaniard was killed at the rock pile I've been talking about, the one where Dr. Kennedy found the first in the series of shaman petroglyphs. So those shaman glyphs he was interested in were most likely the trail markings of that Ute medicine man."

Rivera could feel an excitement rising within him. "I'm going to head out there and see if I can find that rock pile and pick up the shaman trail. It's possible Dr. Kennedy injured himself exploring for the next shaman in the series."

"I'd like to go along. I think I can be of assistance."

Rivera hesitated. "It may not be safe. There was a shooting in that area yesterday morning." Rivera told him about the Zeke Stanton incident.

"Dr. Kennedy and I are very close and I owe him a lot, so I'll risk the danger. Besides, I know what the shaman petroglyphs look like and I have the GPS coordinates of the first three petroglyphs in my notes. Dr. Kennedy gave them to me during one of our discussions. They've never been published. He wanted me to have them in case he died, so I could carry on his work."

"Was he expecting to die?"

"No, no. Nothing like that. It was more like a father leaving something of value to his son. A bequeath. He didn't want his theory to die with him if he happened to pass away. If he couldn't live long enough to prove his critics wrong, he wanted me to do it."

Rivera thought for a long moment about going into the backcountry with a stranger. Ward seemed like a good citizen and Rivera could use some help in finding the petroglyphs, especially from someone who was an expert. But was Ward to be trusted? Perhaps he was the one who had shot Zeke Stanton yesterday. Perhaps he'd even dispatched Dr. Kennedy. "When did you arrive in Moab?"

Ward appeared puzzled by the question. "Last night. I left Salt Lake City yesterday morning and drove down here."

"Can you prove that?"

Ward thought for a moment. "I have a credit card receipt from the motel in Salt Lake City." He thought some more. "I also have a receipt from a gas station in Price." He fished them out of his briefcase and showed them to Rivera.

Rivera read them and checked the dates. Handed them back. "Okay," he said. "Did you bring a daypack?"

"Of course." Ward opened the closet and pulled out a daypack. He checked the contents and refilled the water bottles it contained, then called the office and told the clerk he'd he staying for at least one more day. He looked at Rivera. "I'm ready."

# 9

DURING THE DRIVE to the Big Triangle, Rivera discovered that Harry Ward was a talkative young man. He recounted his life story, about growing up in Redondo Beach, California, and becoming part of the surfer cult. He breezed through college without much effort, lived in a fraternity house, and spent most of his time partying. It wasn't until his senior year in college that he began thinking about the future, wondering what would become of him when the partying was over. During his last semester, he'd taken an anthropology course as an elective and found himself intensely interested in the subject matter. That changed the direction of his life. He entered graduate school at the University of New Mexico to pursue the subject further. His longer-term goal was to get a PhD in anthropology and work with Dr. Kennedy on his petroglyph research.

Rivera enjoyed hearing about Ward's history and his plans for the future. The young man's enthusiasm for life made the deputy smile. Abruptly, Ward stopped talking and opened Rivera's Utah map atlas.

"I'd better shut up and start studying the Big Triangle map," he said. "I need to keep track of where we are."

Rivera splashed across the Dolores River and followed the dirt road to the top of the mesa. He fished his cell phone out of his pocket and called Millie Ives, the dispatcher. He informed her of his plan, told her that Harry Ward was with him, and indicated he'd be out in the Big Triangle all day.

"Okay, Manny. Sheriff Campbell said to tell you he still needs your help on that matter he discussed with you. Said it was priority one. He didn't tell me what he was referring to, but he seemed real anxious about it."

"I understand, Millie. Thanks for the info. Any word on Zeke Stanton's condition?"

"He still hasn't regained consciousness, but his condition is stable and the doctor thinks his chances of pulling through are good."

"That's great news. I need to ask him some questions when he's ready." Rivera thought for a moment, then decided to broach a personal subject with Millie. They had become good friends over the years and she made no secret of the fact that Rivera was her favorite deputy. "Millie, I've got Chris Carey working with me on this case. He's been a big help, but I'm worried about him. Since Rita passed away, his spirits have really sunk. He's been hanging around the house all day and doesn't take care of himself. He needs some conversation and a home cooked meal. You were friends with Rita and know Chris pretty well. Got any suggestions?"

Millie let out a hearty laugh. "You're not very subtle, are you? Okay, Manny, I'll check on him."

"Thanks, Millie." He clicked off and continued driving north across the empty expanse of the Big Triangle until the gate of the McGinty Ranch came into view. He stopped and dialed McGinty's telephone number, but there was no answer. He'd try him again later to see if the rancher had spotted the poachers today.

The road turned east and Rivera continued driving across backcountry now familiar to him. He pointed to the dirt road on his left and the sign that said *Private Drive*. "That's the entrance to the Center for Cosmic Consciousness."

"Huh. It doesn't look like much," said Ward. "I always pictured the Center as kind of a plush resort. Judging by the entrance, I had the wrong impression."

"Don't judge it by its humble entryway. It's actually quite upscale. I think the entrance is understated to discourage visitors. They value their solitude."

"I'd like to see it. I've been curious about where Dr. Kennedy has been living the last couple of years."

"Have you ever met his girlfriend Sheila?"

"Yes. We shared a geology class at the university."

"How well did you know her?"

"Not very well. She was a good student and kind of popular. She seemed to be a hard worker. I spoke with her a couple of times and got the impression she came from poor circumstances. She said her father abandoned her mother and the kids when Sheila was young. She'd always wanted to be the first in her family to get a college degree and become successful."

"She walks with a cane. Do you happen to know how she hurt herself?"

"I never asked her about it but I heard her knee got messed up in an automobile accident."

"Did Dr. Kennedy ever talk about her?"

"No. And that was a topic I never broached with him. I knew he was getting some heat for making advances on a student so I avoided the subject altogether. She was much younger than he was. I was surprised to learn she went with him when he left the university and that the two of them were living together" He shrugged. "I guess if they're happy, why not?"

They continued east, now through terrain unfamiliar to Rivera. Ward continually checked his GPS receiver and Rivera's Utah map atlas. Ward chatted the whole time, talking about Dr. Kennedy's petroglyph theories and how much Ward wanted to be part of his work. From time to time, he would consult something in the file he'd brought along and then jot down some notes. Then he would return to his enthusiastic chatting. Rivera was taking a liking to the young man.

The road passed across sage flats, skirted outcroppings, and dipped and rose at each arroyo crossing.

"You know," said Ward, "we have the coordinates of the first three shaman petroglyphs. I suppose we could save a lot of time if we started at the third shaman and continued west from there. I'd sure like to see them all and take some photographs, but it's probably not necessary."

"I'd like to see them all, too, and not just out of curiosity. It's possible Dr. Kennedy was doing some further study at the first or second shaman site."

"Right. I hadn't thought of that."

Rivera checked his odometer. They were now about seven miles east of the Center.

"We're just now crossing the state line into Colorado," said Ward. He closed the Utah map atlas and opened the one for Colorado. "We need to drive about four more miles. Then we'll have to park and hike south for about a mile."

Soon they entered an area of barren hills separated by scrub brush valleys and dry creek beds. Rivera studied the landscape as they continued east and thought about a time over 200 years ago when Buckskin Charlie Posey walked alone across this rugged terrain with a dead Spaniard's saddlebags slung over his shoulder in order to protect his people from the white man's bad medicine. Rivera wondered what occupied Charlie's thoughts as he left his shaman markings on the rocks. Was he appreciating the vast beauty of this land as he trekked westward, or was he continually preoccupied with the Spanish threat and the danger the interlopers from afar posed to his people? Probably the latter. He must have been a good man, risking his life to protect his people. Rivera wondered if he had a wife and children, where he lived, and what kind of dwelling he inhabited. For some reason, that thought caused Rivera to consider his own situation. He was in his late thirties and still had no family of his own. He felt a recurring sense of time running out and wondered if Gloria Valdez would turn out to be the one with whom he would spend the rest of his life.

Ward interrupted his thoughts. "Stop here. Time to hike."

Rivera pulled off to the side of the road. The two men grabbed their daypacks and headed south over the hills and through the shallow valleys. The air was cool and crystal clear, and the breeze brought with it a faint scent of sage. The cloudless sky was a dark shade of blue and the sun, now halfway up the sky, warmed the left side of Rivera's back. The LaSal Mountains rose ahead of them in the distance, its twelve-thousand-foot peaks covered with a fresh dusting of bright white snow. Rivera found himself squinting due to the brilliance of the sunlight reflecting off the snow. He put on his sunglasses.

As they hiked through the grass, sage, and wildflowers, a lone, shiny black raven perched on a rock croaked at the intruders entering its domain. Rivera wondered if

the bird was objecting to their presence or was just trying to make friendly conversation. He'd found himself
in proximity to a raven more than once when he was
alone in the backcountry. He remembered how some
of the large birds seemed to enjoy human company and
the sound of the human voice. A couple of times, he'd
gotten as close as five feet to a lone raven, sat down,
and talked to the creature. The birds didn't fly off in
fear. Rather, they seemed to enjoy the companionship,
like two solo hikers encountering each other in some
remote spot in the high desert, exchanging stories for
a while to break the feeling of aloneness, and then
heading their separate ways.

As the hikers passed over the last rise in the terrain, they could now see a cluster of large rocks in the
distance.

Ward pointed. "Look! That must be it."

Rivera studied the rocks. From a distance, they
didn't appear particularly interesting—just a pile of
large rocks out in the middle of some high mesa land.

He noticed Ward was picking up the pace now,
obviously excited by the prospect of finding the first
petroglyph in the series. Rivera picked up his pace
too, feeling a sense of anticipation as they approached
their first goal. He wondered how many other human
beings had ever visited this site. Besides the ones who
had inscribed the petroglyphs on the rock surfaces
and the early Utes who had visited the site during the

winter solstice for luck in their hunts, probably there had not been many. Rivera was eager to inspect the winter solstice indicator and also to see if he could identify the place where the old Ute had killed the Spanish conquistador. Then a thought occurred to him. Was the rock the Ute had used as a weapon still there, lying on the ground?

As they drew closer, they approached the rock pile with a kind of silent reverence. After all, it was once considered a holy place by the Utes. Rivera figured that since the Utes were later confined to reservation land some distance away, they probably didn't visit this site anymore.

They arrived at the rock pile. Rivera circled the site, looking to see if there was a trail leading to it or a campsite or any indication of human visitation. He found none.

"Over here," shouted Ward from the other side of the rock pile. "Over here." There was excitement in his voice like a little boy catching his first fish.

Rivera circled around to where Ward was standing. The young anthropologist was wearing a big grin and pointing at the flat face of an enormous slab of red rock covered with a patina of black desert varnish. It was a petroglyph panel about seven feet high and fifteen feet wide. On it were inscribed well over a hundred petroglyphs. There were dozens of shamans, animal figures, wavy lines, spirals, and rows of dots. These, Rivera figured, were left by the Fremont people and the Utes. Two figures depicting men on horseback were obviously left by the Utes after the time when the Spaniards had arrived and introduced horses to the Americas. Off to one side of the panel was an array of crucifixes surrounding an image of the Holy Mother. No doubt this had been inscribed by the Spaniards. At the bottom were two names likely carved in the rock by cowboys, each with a date: *Amos Bass, Dec 12, 1932* and *F.R. Hixson, April 16, 1921.*

After Ward took a couple of dozen photographs, he explained to Rivera how to tell the Fremont petroglyphs from the Ute petroglyphs. Then he then pointed to a shaman figure, not on the panel, but farther around to one side of the rock pile. The shaman's left arm was at its side and its right arm was extended straight out. "Look, there it is. The beginning of Dr. Kennedy's shaman trail." He took a series of close-up photographs, as did Rivera.

"Why do you suppose this one isn't on the panel with the rest of the petroglyphs?" asked Rivera.

"Because its arm had to point in exactly the right direction. Don't forget, each shaman points to the next shaman in the series. And, of course, they are two-dimensional images, so the old Ute had to move around the rock pile to a place where the shaman's arm would be pointing in the correct azimuth."

Rivera inspected the markings carefully, remembering it was the micro grooves in the cuts that had made

Kennedy believe the petroglyphs in the series were all inscribed by the same man. Then he circled the rock pile. He smiled when he spotted the most likely place the Spaniard had sat down to rest. It was a sandy spot at the base of a nearly vertical slab of smooth rock where a man could sit on the soft ground, rest his back against the rock, and relax. After some searching, Rivera found a place on the opposite side of the rock pile where the old Ute could have climbed up to a vantage point about fifteen feet directly above the Spaniard. From there, a large rock thrown down on an unsuspecting soldier would be lethal. Rivera returned to the place where the Spaniard had been sitting, his eyes scanning the ground. He spotted a large, ovoid-shaped rock encrusted with patches of orange, gray, and light green lichens. It was lying half buried in the soil. There it was—the weapon of the legend.

He could see no sign of the Spaniard's bones or armor. Probably his fellow countrymen had later found his body and buried him somewhere.

Rivera imagined now that he could see the whole episode unfolding—the Ute medicine man collecting herbs near the rock pile, looking up and seeing the Conquistador in the distance, headed his way. The Ute then hiding behind the rocks. Rivera pictured the Spaniard approaching from the north, slowly crossing the same terrain that he and Ward had just traversed. The Spaniard, wearing armor glistening in the sun and carrying a sword and a lance, approached on horseback, arrived at the rock pile, and dismounted for a rest in the shade. Rivera pictured him sitting down and removing his helmet while the Ute, hiding on the other side of the rock pile, grasped that very ovoid-shaped rock and climbed up to a place directly above the Spaniard. Then he took careful aim—a miss would mean certain death for the Ute—and flung the rock down on the unwitting Spaniard's head with all his might. He imagined the adrenalin-charged emotions the Ute must have felt just before and just after the rock had struck its target.

Rivera glanced at his watch. It was a little after ten thirty. "We'd better get going," he said. "How far is it to the next petroglyph?"

"About a mile," said Ward.

Rivera was thinking about his vehicle. He didn't want to end up miles away from it at the end of the day and then have to hike all the way back. "How far is petroglyph number two from the road?"

"It's a lot closer than this one. I'd say about three hundred yards."

"Let's go back to my pickup and we'll drive over there as close as we can get."

"Okay," said Ward, "but first, look at the direction the shaman is pointing. You can see a high point in the landscape about a mile away. That's probably where the next shaman is located. Remember, there's line-of-sight visibility from one shaman to the next. That's not easy to accomplish in this terrain. The Ute medicine man had been very careful about where he placed the shaman petroglyphs."

Just before departing, Rivera looked for and found the spiral petroglyph and the slot in the rocks that the early Utes used to identify the day of the winter solstice. He and Ward took photographs and both felt a palpable connection with those who had visited this sacred site centuries ago.

They hiked back to Rivera's pickup, made a U-turn, and drove back in the direction from which they had come. Ward talked excitedly about their adventure the whole time. Rivera was also enjoying it, but he saw the possibility of a full day of hiking and searching ahead of them. He hoped Ward was in shape for it.

Ward was engrossed in studying the map and checking the GPS receiver as they drove. After several minutes, he pointed. "We should park right about here."

Rivera pulled over and they hiked south toward a rise in the terrain. After some searching, they found it. The second shaman had been inscribed by the Ute on a rock outcropping at the top of the rise. They found no other petroglyphs in the immediate area. The shaman pointed to another rise in the terrain about three-quarters of a mile to the west. They took photographs and walked back to Rivera's vehicle.

They found the third shaman petroglyph with no trouble. It was a few hundred yards south of the road. Knowing the GPS coordinates made finding the first three shaman petroglyphs easy. Rivera realized that finding the next one would be more difficult, since, from here on, they did not know the coordinates of the petroglyphs. The third shaman pointed west, just like the others. In the distance, he could see a pronounced knoll on an upslope about a mile and a half away. He judged that would be where they would find shaman number four.

They returned to Rivera's pickup, drove west on the dirt road, and hiked to the knoll. After fifteen minutes of searching, they found the fourth petroglyph. They photographed it, recorded its GPS coordinates, and returned to the pickup. They headed west on the road and now re-crossed the state line back into Utah.

# 10

FOUR HOURS LATER, they were several miles farther west, and the terrain was becoming more and more rugged and rocky. They were now searching for shaman number ten in the series. The first nine glyphs were more or less laid out in line heading west and then bending to the west-northwest. The current segment was taking them across to the north side of BLM Route 107. For Rivera, the excitement of finding another shaman figure had waned, and his leg muscles were getting sore. The trekking had long since transitioned from a fun adventure to hard work. The afternoon sun beat down on them and Rivera was feeling the extra pounds he'd put on. Ward's youth and enthusiasm kept his spirits high and he showed no signs of fatigue. Maybe eating salads for lunch wasn't such a bad idea.

As they crossed the road, Rivera saw a gray pickup truck parked a hundred yards farther down the road. He wondered if that was the truck McGinty had seen when he spotted two men carrying a bighorn ram's head out of the rocks. He inspected the truck with his binoculars, noting it had Colorado plates. He jotted down the license number. He tried calling McGinty again to see if he'd seen the poachers, but there was still no answer. He could wait here and see if the poachers returned to the truck, but there were lots of gray pickup trucks in the world. He decided to push on. For now, having the license plate number would suffice. Rivera parked his vehicle well off the road and hidden in a cluster of junipers. If the gray truck belonged to the poachers, he didn't want them to know that law enforcement was in the area and scare them off to another bighorn hunting ground. He wanted them right where he could find them.

Rivera and Ward continued the search. Ward was still acting like a kid in a candy store. He was ahead of Rivera, his enthusiastic stride undiminished by the miles of difficult hiking. If anything, he'd become more energized the farther they went. And he was good at finding the best way through the rocks and brush. At each shaman site, he chatted about the discovery, took copious photographs, and carefully recorded the GPS coordinates in his notebook.

They continued hiking toward the next landmark, a red rock spire that rose high above the surrounding rocks. Rivera thought again about the old Ute, imagining him trekking through these very same rocks over two hundred years ago. Then he imagined Dr. Kennedy following the same route. Rivera could almost feel the anthropologist's excitement as he discovered each successive shaman in the series, all the while plotting how he might use the information to silence his critics. To Rivera, Kennedy seemed like an interesting but complex man. Why had he given up and left the university to live in a remote off-the-grid cabin at the Center for Cosmic Consciousness? Had he become fed up with the criticism and decided to withdraw from his critics? Had he wanted a place where he could take his young girlfriend without critical eyes judging him? Or had he found incontrovertible proof of his theory in this remote backcountry and was organizing his scientific data for a blockbuster paper that would crush his critics and return him to the pinnacle of the anthropology community?

They moved deeper and deeper into the rocks, Rivera recalling McGinty's ominous words of caution. *Be careful out in them rocks. You're a sitting duck for a rifle shot.* He hoped he wasn't taking Ward into a dangerous situation.

Forty minutes later, Rivera and Ward reached the spire. Rivera reckoned they were now due north of the Center. They searched for fifteen minutes around the base of the monolith but found nothing. Rivera took off his hat, wiped the sweat off his forehead with his shirtsleeve, and returned the hat to his head. He was growing weary. The thrill of the hunt had long since worn off.

Ward kept circling the spire. "I don't understand it," he said. "It's got to be here somewhere. This spire was definitely what that last shaman petroglyph was pointing to. And this is the highest point we could see from where we were standing."

"Let's sit for a minute and rest," said Rivera. "Collect our thoughts. Think about where we might have gone wrong." He selected a shady spot at the base of the spire, sat down, and leaned back against the rock. His eyes scanned the horizon, McGinty's words of caution echoing in his mind. They were located at the head of a small canyon that led downward and to the west. To the north, the terrain became even rockier and he could see sheer cliffs in the distance.

Ward sat down, looking despondent. "Kind of a bummer, isn't it?"

"Don't worry," Rivera said. "It's got to be around here somewhere. Let's just relax for a few minutes." At that moment, he heard a loud crack that echoed off the surrounding rock faces. "Watch it," he said. "Get down."

They scrambled away from the spire into a cluster of red rock boulders near the head of the canyon. Rivera drew his Glock, now kicking himself for bringing a civilian along. "Keep your head down," he said as he took off his hat and peered over one of the rocks. He saw nothing—no movement, no reflections, no gunman. Then he heard another crack and another series of echoes. Rivera had heard many gunshots over the years—handguns at the firing range, rifles and pistols out in open country, even a few shots fired in his direction. But this sound was different. He couldn't place it. Then he noticed movement on top of the cliff to the north. Two bighorn rams were facing each other. They were magnificent specimens—large solidly built frames, tan in color, pale muscular rumps, short legs, and large circular horns. They stood ten feet apart, sizing each other up. Then, simultaneously, they rose up on their hind legs, coiled up the muscles in their bodies, and charged each other. Their heads smashed together violently with a loud crack. Rivera holstered his weapon and relaxed. It was the rutting season and the males were competing for the ewes in the herd.

Rivera and Ward sat there, staring up at the two rams through binoculars. The rams again stood ten feet apart, facing each other and girding themselves for the next round of combat. Their heads were held high, their stances regal, and their amber-colored eyes seemed to embody determination and confidence. They were preparing themselves for the next charge.

"Look at them," said Ward. "Such magnificent creatures. I wish I'd brought a telephoto lens."

Rivera nodded. "I don't see how anyone could kill a bighorn."

As he stood up, Rivera noticed a shaman figure inscribed on one of the rocks behind which they had been crouching. It was located just where the terrain began its downward slope into the small canyon. The shaman's arm pointed toward the canyon.

"Look, Harry. There it is," he said. "I guess the old Ute couldn't find a place on the spire that was as good as this one."

Ward's excitement and his smile returned. "Let's go," he said.

They began hiking into the canyon, carefully inspecting each rock surface for the next shaman petroglyph. The canyon started out narrow with a steep slope. After a half mile, the terrain began to level out and the distance between the canyon walls widened. Soon they were in a flat area populated with sagebrush, junipers, and a few cottonwood trees. As they proceeded farther, they emerged from the foliage only for Rivera to discover that he had reached the site of the Zeke Stanton shooting—but this time he'd arrived from the opposite direction.

"I'll be damned," he said. "This is the place where Zeke Stanton was shot."

Ward thought for a long moment. "Maybe that's not a coincidence," he said.

Rivera now took a new interest in the large rocks which had fallen from the cliff faces over the millennia and the cliff faces themselves. It took twenty minutes of searching, but Rivera finally located a shaman figure inscribed at the base of the south facing wall. It was about a hundred feet from the spot where Stanton had been shot. The petroglyph was the same as the other figures they'd been following, except this shaman wasn't pointing outward. Both arms were at its sides. This must be where the old Ute had hidden the saddlebags, thought Rivera. He looked around, now wishing he'd brought along a shovel.

Ward was circling the area, ecstatic they'd found the last shaman. He was taking photographs and chattering about the saddlebags and what kind of white man's bad medicine they might contain. "I've never seen bad medicine before," he said with laughter, "unless you count that cheap tequila I drank in Tijuana."

Rivera had mixed emotions. He was glad they'd found the last shaman in the series but disappointed that he hadn't found Dr. Kennedy. He stood back from the shaman and surveyed the area. His eyes fell upon the cliff wall itself. Like most red rock cliffs, the walls were sheer in places and in other places had vertical corrugations. Near the shaman was a corrugation that looked like thousands of others he'd seen in the canyon country. The opening for this one was only about three feet wide, but appeared to widen as it went deeper into the red rock. From where he was standing, Rivera couldn't tell how far back it went. He wanted to enter for a closer inspection but the entrance was blocked by a dense, nine-foot-high barberry bush with stiff, gray-green leaves, each leaf edged with tiny, sharp spines. Not the kind of bush a deer would want to munch on.

Pushing the bush aside and squeezing between it and the wall to gain entry would be, Rivera knew from experience, an unpleasant and bloody experience.

He noticed a crawl space below the bush adjacent to the left wall. As he studied it, he noticed what appeared to be brush marks in the sandy bottom, suggesting someone or something had crawled through there recently. It had to be within the last few days because the wind in the canyon hadn't quite smoothed over the edges of the depressions.

Rivera took off his hat and hung it on the branch of a nearby pinyon pine. "I'm going in there and have a look around," he said. He got down on his knees, then his belly, and began inching forward under the bush. When his head and shoulders were safely past the far side of the bush, he cautiously raised his head. The first thing he saw was a pith helmet lying upside down in the sand. The second was the body of a man.

"Did you find anything back there?" asked Ward in a loud voice.

Rivera shinnied the rest of the way under the bush and stood up in what seemed like a red rock hallway. The opening tapered to a dead end about ten feet back. He extracted the wallet from the corpse's pocket and checked the driver's license. The dead man was Dr. Peter Kennedy. A cursory inspection revealed a gunshot wound to the chest. "Harry, I'm afraid I've got some bad news," Rivera said. "I found Dr. Kennedy. He's dead. It looks like he's been shot."

"Oh, God, no. I'm coming in there."

"No," said Rivera in a stern voice. "This is a crime scene. You stay out." He checked his cell phone. There were no bars. "You can do something for me, though. I can't get a cell phone signal in here. Back away from this wall until you get a signal and call this number." He gave Ward the number for Millie Ives. Rivera was sure there was a signal available in the center of the canyon because he'd made a call from there yesterday. "Tell the dispatcher where I am. Give her the GPS coordinates. Tell her it's close to where I found Zeke Stanton yesterday. Tell her about Dr. Kennedy and ask her to dispatch the Medical Examiner and the mortuary people. And make sure she tells them to bring a machete to bushwhack this thorny barberry at the entrance."

"Okay, Deputy Rivera. Will do." Ward's voice cracked, as though he were on the verge of crying. Knowing how close Ward and Dr. Kennedy had been, Rivera now wished he hadn't barked out orders to the young man in such an abrupt manner.

Rivera heard Ward's footfalls as he walked away and then his voice speaking in the distance. While Ward made the call, Rivera used his cell phone to take photographs of the crime scene. He took pictures of the body and the two sets of footprints in the sand. One set was made by hiking boots with a checkered sole that matched the boots Kennedy was wearing. The other set was made by larger boots which had a sole pattern of wavy lines and ellipses. Rivera assumed those belonged to the shooter.

As he was photographing the scene, Rivera noticed a narrow opening in the red rock wall on the right side of the room. It was about twenty inches wide and led back about eight feet where it dead ended. The opening wouldn't have been noticeable when viewed by someone in the canyon proper because it would likely appear to be a shadow on the wall. He stepped closer to the opening, examining it. Both sets of boot prints led into the opening and then back out. The shooters prints stepped on Dr. Kennedy's prints, so the shooter had entered the opening after Dr. Kennedy had gone in and come back out. Rivera carefully photographed the prints, then entered the space. Near the end of the passageway, he noticed handholds leading up the wall on his left. His gaze followed them up about thirty feet where they ended at the edge of an alcove overlooking the room where Kennedy's body lay.

"Harry, there are some handholds in here leading up to what appears to be an ancient cliff dwelling. I'm going to climb up there and have a look. If you hear a loud thump, call the medics."

"It's probably an Ancestral Puebloan cliff dwelling," said Ward. "It wouldn't be a Fremont dwelling. They tended to live in pit houses or wickiups. I'd like to come in and take a look at it."

"You'll have to wait for another day, Harry—when it's no longer a crime scene."

"Okay, I understand. Well, be careful up there."

Rivera began climbing up the hand holds. They were notches chiseled out of the soft sandstone many centuries ago by someone using a handheld tool made of harder rock. The Ancestral Puebloans, or Anasazi as they were once called, built their dwellings so they could easily be defended. An attacker coming up the handholds wouldn't have a chance against someone standing above with a spear or a large rock. Rivera had climbed handholds before. He knew it was dangerous because windblown sand tended to accumulate in the handholds, possibly causing a hand or foot to slip. It was necessary to sweep each handhold clean as the climber advanced.

Without looking down, Rivera ascended the cliff face one handhold at a time. When he neared the halfway point, he knew any slip could have serious consequences. The possibility of a broken back crossed his mind. He set that thought aside and concentrated on securing a firm grasp on each handhold as he advanced. Finally, he reached the top. There, he crawled over the edge and into an eight-foot deep alcove in the red rock. The alcove, like many others Rivera had seen in the canyon country, was a cave-like formation created when layers of soft rock weathered faster than the harder rock above it. It overlooked the small room where Dr. Kennedy's body lay. Centuries ago, its inhabitants had closed off the alcove with a wall constructed of stacked rocks mortared with mud. A one-foot square opening in the wall served as a window and allowed light to enter. He stood up, hunched over beneath the five-foot ceiling, and noticed what appeared to be the remnant of a yucca fiber sandal protruding from the dirt and blow sand on the floor of the room.

At the far end of the room, a small doorway connected to another room. Rivera squeezed through the doorway. The second room, larger than the first, had a scattering of tiny corn cobs on the floor and a large window which allowed him to carefully lean out and see Dr. Kennedy's body in the sand below. Another doorway led to a third room which contained a cracked gray ceramic pot with a white sawtooth pattern around the neck. Rivera pictured a family or two living in these quarters long ago and wondered for a moment what their life had been like.

In the back of the third room, he saw two parallel depressions in the dirt floor. Each was about eighteen inches long and six inches wide. The color of the dirt within the depressions was darker than the floor of the room, suggesting to Rivera that something which had been resting on that spot for a very long time had recently been removed. He stared at the shape of the indentations, realizing they could easily have been made by saddlebags.

# 11

RIVERA SAT AT his desk, sipping on a mug of coffee, his third of the morning. He'd checked the license plate of the gray pickup he'd seen parked on the side of BLM Route 107. Turned out it belonged to an elderly couple who owned and operated a bookstore in Grand Junction. He'd visited the store with Amy Rousseau a couple of years ago and met them. In no way did they strike him as bighorn sheep poachers. They were probably out exploring the backcountry or collecting rocks.

Rivera yawned and leaned back in his chair. Through his office window, he saw in the distance a yellow and black hot-air balloon slowly drifting over Wilson Mesa. His eyes followed the craft until it disappeared from view. His leg muscles were still tight from yesterday's hike, and he took a moment to massage his calves. He'd been up late last night, finishing his investigation at the crime scene and writing his report while everything was still fresh in his mind. Dr. Pudge Devlin, vintner of fine Merlot wines in Castle Valley and part-time Medical Examiner for Grand County, had arrived at the crime scene around sunset. He'd examined the victim, pronounced him dead, and told Rivera he'd begin the autopsy as soon as the body was moved to the hospital. Harry Ward had requested and received permission to return to Moab in the mortuary vehicle with his deceased mentor.

Rivera had emptied the contents of Dr. Peter Kennedy's pockets, bagging and tagging each item. Besides the man's wallet, there was a set of vehicle keys, a handkerchief, and a small GPS receiver. The waypoints stored in the receiver corresponded to the locations of the shaman figures Rivera and Harry Ward had found. The wallet contained a few hundred dollars in cash, a driver's license, a Visa credit card, a medical insurance card, and a photograph of Kennedy and Sheila holding hands in front of their cabin. In his shirt pocket was a notebook containing sketches of petroglyphs and related notations. In the sand next to the body, Rivera had found a small, expensive digital camera. He'd scrolled through the photographs stored in the camera and found nothing but images of petroglyphs and backcountry scenes. Kennedy's daypack contained a spare battery pack for the camera, a two-liter bottle of water, a sack of trail mix, an assortment of snack bars, and a folded topographic map of the Big Triangle. Rivera inspected the map for markings but found none.

After Rivera had left the crime scene, he'd driven to the Center for Cosmic Consciousness and informed

Brother Timothy Pierce of Dr. Kennedy's death. Pierce was visibly upset and dumbstruck, and reverted to old habits by making the sign of the cross over and over. After leaving Pierce's office, Rivera glanced through the window and noticed the former priest extracting a liquor bottle from a cabinet.

Next, Rivera had driven back to the off-the-grid cabin and broken the news to Sheila. Sheila had stood there quivering, a look of disbelief on her face. She began to wobble but managed with the help of her cane to sit down on the cabin's front steps. She buried her face in her hands and cried. Rivera felt awful. Informing people that a loved one was dead was the one part of his job he wished he could avoid.

"Oh, poor Peter," she'd said between sobs. "He was my whole life. What am I going to do now?"

After delivering the bad news to Sheila, Rivera had searched through Kennedy's personal things in the cabin. He'd found nothing pertinent to the case. He'd picked up the man's laptop and taken it with him.

Now Rivera sat at his desk, paging through the files stored on Kennedy's laptop. There were hundreds of pages of technical material, papers written by him and others in the field of anthropology. Curiously, there wasn't much else. No games, no social media, no news sites, no favorites, no email account. With no connection to the internet, the computer had been used solely for word processing and document storage. As far as

Rivera could tell, the computer contained no information that would help him identify the shooter.

Last night, Dr. Devlin had sent Rivera the bullet he'd removed from Kennedy's chest. Rivera sent a messenger with that bullet and the one removed from Stanton to the State Crime Lab in Price, Utah. An expedited analysis was requested. The results had come back early this morning. The two .38 caliber bullets had been fired from the same gun.

Rivera was tumbling the facts around in his mind when Dr. Devlin came into his office. He was a short, stocky man with a paunchy stomach and a florid face. Rivera had worked several cases with Devlin over the past six years and the two had become good friends. Devlin had a subtle sense of humor that Rivera always enjoyed. He'd been a general practitioner in Denver with a highly successful practice, but one day decided to opt for a slower life. With more than enough money in his bank account, he sold his practice, bought a house and five acres in Castle Valley just upriver from Moab, and began planting a vineyard. Growing grapes and fermenting wine turned out to be more work than he'd realized, but it was a labor of love. Now, Devlin was well known in Moab for his Porcupine Rim Merlot. The wine was in high demand by the locals but its supply was limited because Devlin consumed most of the product himself. He'd accepted the job as part-time Medical Examiner only because his services would rarely be required and because it gave him a way to keep his hand in medicine without interfering too much with his winemaking.

Devlin placed a basket of clothing on Rivera's desk. Resting on top were a pith helmet and a pair of hiking boots. "Here are Kennedy's personals. That bullet I gave you last night was the cause of death. Punctured his heart. He died instantly." Devlin sat down and looked at Rivera with a wry smile. He had a self-satisfied look on his face. "You're the one that searched the body, right?"

"That's right."

"And you consider yourself to be pretty good at searching bodies?"

Rivera sat back. He knew he must have overlooked something. He also knew Devlin wouldn't reveal it without first running him through a wringer. "Well, I'm not perfect, Pudge. There's always a tiny chance I missed something."

"And if someone were to point out your error, keeping said egregious dereliction to himself forevermore, would that someone be entitled to a small reward?"

Rivera smiled. "How small a reward are we talking about?"

Devlin sat back in his chair, took off his glasses, fogged them with his breath, and wiped them with the shirttail that was hanging out of his pants. He held the glasses up to the light and inspected them, milking the moment for all it was worth. "Chris Carey mentioned that you bought him dinner at Pasta Jay's."

"Alright, dinner at Pasta Jay's. But this has to be good. And useful."

"No, no, no. No conditions. You'll just have to trust my judgment."

Rivera smiled. "You know, Pudge, I could arrest you for withholding evidence. And our jail-keeper doesn't serve wine."

Devlin laughed and pulled a clear plastic bag from his shirt pocket. "I found this inside Kennedy's pith helmet. I'd seen those helmets in the movies before but I'd never seen one in real life, so I was taking a close look at it. I spotted a small compartment inside the lining. It looked like a homemade pocket someone had sewn in there. It had a flap that allowed you to Velcro it shut. Inside the compartment was a damn coin. Looks pretty old. I think it's gold." He handed the bag to Rivera.

Rivera held the bag up to the light and studied the coin. Turned it over and studied the other side. "You just got yourself a dinner at Pasta Jay's."

"What is that thing? It looks like some kind of foreign coin."

"Yeah. Spanish, maybe," said Rivera. He was thinking about the old story of the Ute medicine man and the Spanish Conquistador. He turned to his computer and Googled *coins, Spanish, gold*. A few clicks later, an array of coins was displayed on his monitor. "Looks like it's an old Spanish doubloon."

"Probably worth some money," said Devlin.

Rivera nodded. "Yeah, I'll bet. I need to find a coin expert who can tell me more about this." He picked up the telephone on his desk and punched in Chris Carey's number.

"Hello?"

"Chris, it's Manny.

"Hey, Manny." There was a note of enthusiasm in Carey's voice.

"Do you know of someone who's an expert in old coins? Maybe a coin dealer in Grand Junction?"

"You don't have to go that far. There's a guy down in Monticello. Older guy, retired now. He had a coin shop in San Francisco years ago. The shop is long gone but he still buys and sells coins for his own account. His name's Nick Van Zandt. Just a minute, I've got his phone number right here." After a short delay, Carey read the number off. "Tell Nick I sent you."

"Thanks, Chris." Rivera started to hang up.

"By the way, Manny, you'll never guess what happened last night."

"What happened?"

"Millie Ives, your dispatcher, gave me a call." Rivera could hear Carey smiling. "She invited me over to her place for dinner tonight."

# 12

AN HOUR LATER, Rivera was in Monticello, standing at the door of a large brick home shaded by four spruce trees. Wrought iron bars protected the windows and a security camera was mounted above the door. He knocked, surprised at how solid the door felt. Soon, he heard locks being unlocked. A man who appeared to be in his eighties pulled the door ajar and peered out. He studied Rivera for a long moment, then cast his gaze around the front yard and out into the street.

Finally, he smiled. "You must be Deputy Rivera."

Rivera nodded. "Thanks for seeing me on such short notice. Chris Carey said you might be able to help me with a question."

"Of course. Come in and have a seat." He pulled the door all the way open and gestured Rivera inside.

The first things Rivera noticed were the three display cases along the walls of the entry hallway. In the first was a collection of museum-quality, Ancestral Puebloan ceramic pots that Rivera knew was worth a lot of money. He'd become acquainted with many of the pot types years ago. His first murder case as a Grand County deputy had involved a long-forgotten, remote cave containing a valuable collection of Native American pots and figurines worth over a half million dollars.

The second display case contained a collection of arrowheads and spear points, and the third contained nine expensive Hopi kachina figures.

"I collect things," said Van Zandt with a British accent. He spoke slowly with an exaggerated diction and his chin tilted upward. He was about six feet three inches tall with a large girth and a bald head. He reminded Rivera of Alfred Hitchcock. He wore a short sleeve, white dress shirt and his baggy khaki pants were belted high on top of his stomach. He peered at Rivera through thick glasses.

"Very impressive collections," said Rivera, as he sat down on one end of an expensive couch with silk upholstery.

"I also collect stamps, but coins are my specialty. I've made a living off of them my entire life." He sat down at the other end of the couch and wasted no time with chitchat. "You said you had a coin you'd like me to look at?"

"Yes, if you wouldn't mind." Rivera fished the bagged coin out of his shirt pocket and handed it to Van Zandt. "What can you tell me about this one?"

"May I remove it from the bag?"

"Sure."

Van Zandt extracted the coin, holding it by its edges between his thumb and forefinger. "Ah, a Spanish doubloon. It's gold, of course. And in very good condition." He held it out for Rivera to see and pointed. "The front side displays the Hapsburg family shield since Spain was ruled by the Hapsburgs when this coin was minted." He turned it over. "On the obverse side is a Crusader cross, a symbol of Catholicism which the Spaniards were determined to spread across the globe. This coin is probably worth twenty-five hundred dollars at wholesale. Do you know anything about the history of Spanish coins in America?"

Rivera shrugged. "Nothing at all."

"It's all quite interesting. The Spaniards arrived in North America in the 1500s and pretty much had their way until the early 1800s when Mexico drove them out. During that roughly three-hundred-year period, they dominated Mexico and what is now the southwest part of the United States. As I'm sure you know, they came for two primary reasons: to impose their culture, religion, language, and social mores on the New World, and take for the Spanish Crown whatever valuable commodities they could lay their hands on. Gold, of course, was the most desired commodity."

Rivera had never thought much about the evolution of currencies in America but now found himself genuinely interested. He wondered how the gold taken from the indigenous peoples had been transformed into coins. "Did they take the gold bullion back to Spain, use it to mint coins, and then transport the coins back to America?"

"Actually most of the coins used here were minted here. As commerce began to establish itself in the New World and a currency was needed, they simply converted the gold they acquired into doubloons. They would heat the gold to make it malleable, hammer it out into flat sheets, and cut out circular blanks. Then, using a hammer and crude, hard metal dies, they would imprint the blanks with a Hapsburg shield or a Crusader cross, or both. The coins were then trimmed to the proper weight. Doubloons eventually became the de facto currency in much of the Americas."

"Really? How long were they in circulation here?"

"Longer than most people would guess. Each of the thirteen colonies issued its own paper currency which was susceptible to ultra-inflation, so gold doubloons and other foreign precious-metal coins became the preferred currencies. Later, after the United States was formed and despite the existence of a stable U.S. currency, doubloons were still in circulation here as late as the 1850s. They were the most trusted currency on the continent. Would you mind if I took a photograph of this coin for my files?"

"Not at all."

Van Zandt left the room and returned with a camera. He placed the coin under a lamp on an end table and photographed both sides. Then he lowered his bulk back onto the couch. "May I ask how this coin came to be in your possession?"

Rivera considered the question. He could think of no reason not to tell Van Zandt about Dr. Kennedy. "A man was shot and killed two days ago in the backcountry east of the LaSal Mountains. He was carrying this coin in a secret compartment in the pith helmet he was wearing."

Van Zandt sat up straight, a stunned look on his face. "A pith helmet, you say? Was that man's name Peter Kennedy?"

Now it was Rivera's turn to be surprised. "Yes, it was. I take it you knew him."

He nodded. "I've known him for a couple of years. During that time, he visited me about twice a month. He was killed, you say? How terrible. He was a good chap."

"Were you friends?"

"Not really. I liked him but I wouldn't characterize him as a friend. We had more of a business relationship."

"What kind of business?"

"Each time he visited, he brought me a single gold doubloon. He'd always make a big production of removing it from the secret compartment in that absurd pith helmet he wore. I don't know why he didn't just carry the coin in his pocket. The doubloons were denominated in one, two, four, or eight escudos. Each time he came, he'd sell me the coin for its wholesale price. We'd check my numismatic catalog to be sure the price was fair. Some of the coins, the ones in excellent condition, were worth as much as ten thousand dollars apiece."

"How did you pay him? In cash?"

"Oh, no. After we agreed on a price, we'd go to my bank here in Monticello. At his request, I'd have them issue him a half dozen cashier's checks in various amounts from my account. Each time, he asked that the checks be made out to his favorite charitable organizations, and, of course, I complied with his wishes—it made no difference to me. Then we'd drive to the post office and he would mail off the checks. The oddest thing was that he sent the donations anonymously. He didn't even put a return address on the envelopes."

"Wait a minute. Are you saying he kept none of the money for himself?"

"Occasionally, he'd pocket a few hundred dollars in cash to cover his living expenses, but the bulk of the money was donated to the charities he supported."

Rivera considered that. "Makes sense, I guess. He spent most of his time in the backcountry looking for petroglyphs to support his theories about the Fremont people and the Utes. And he lived off the grid. So I don't suppose he needed much money for daily living expenses."

"He told me once that he wanted to keep his life simple. So almost all the money he received from selling me the coins went to charity."

"What kind of charities was he supporting?"

"All of them were related to college scholarship programs. He said helping deserving kids get an education was the best thing he could do with the money."

"Did he ever talk about where the coins came from?"

"During one of his visits, after we'd conducted our business, we had a few libations and he loosened up a bit. He told me some things he probably wouldn't have mentioned if he'd been completely sober. Of course, his secret was safe with me I would never have shared it with anyone because I wanted the coins to keep coming. He said he'd found a large cache of gold coins out in that Big Triangle country. He wanted to convert them into cash and put the money to good use before someone else found them. And he wanted the conversion to take place slowly over time so no one would notice. He emphasized that he didn't want the wealth to affect his lifestyle. He and his girlfriend lived a simple uncluttered life."

"You mean Sheila?"

"Yes, that's what he called her."

"Did you ever meet her?"

"No, he always came alone."

"Did he mention any specifics about where he'd found the cache? Anything at all?"

Van Zandt laughed. "No. And I didn't ask."

"Do you know if Sheila knew about the cache?"

"He said he'd told her about it right after he found it. That was when he was still at the university. I got the feeling he was a little insecure about keeping her, given the difference in their ages and the fact that he wasn't getting any younger. He thought her knowledge of the cache would bind her a little closer to him. He said she'd come from a poor family and was always concerned about financial security."

"And she wouldn't be able to follow him to the cache because of her handicap, so she'd never have direct access to the wealth," said Rivera, almost to himself.

"Yes, he mentioned she walked with a cane."

"That's interesting about the cashier's checks. So there was never any record of the transactions that could be traced back to him."

"That's right. Perhaps it was some sort of tax avoidance scheme. The government has a claim on all treasure found on land or sea."

"How big a claim?" asked Rivera.

Van Zandt laughed. "Between state and federal taxes, they'll take almost half of it. And that's true whether you sell it or keep it."

# 13

DURING THE DRIVE back to Moab, Rivera thought a great deal about Dr. Peter Kennedy. Despite his overbearing manner, he must have been an exceptional human being. To Rivera's way of thinking, most people, if they'd suddenly come into substantial wealth, wouldn't choose to donate it to those in need. Instead, they'd be buying new houses and new cars and traveling first class around the world. Rivera wished he'd have known the man. Besides being generous, he'd led a most interesting life. He was someone Rivera would gladly have called a friend.

When Rivera walked into his office, he found Adam Dunne waiting for him with a confused look on his face.

"I'm back in town," said Dunne. "I just returned from Bears Ears National Monument. Washington is considering reversing its designation as a monument, so the Secretary of the Interior was touring the area with some other bigwigs. Of course, there was a group of demonstrators there who were opposed to the change. People are plenty sore and I don't blame them. The last thing we need there are mineral extraction activities destroying those priceless Native American ruins. I was there to help keep the peace. Anyway, when I got back in town, I learned about the Dr. Kennedy business. I don't understand what's going on. Why were Zeke Stanton and this Dr. Kennedy fellow shot? Is poaching bighorn sheep so lucrative that men will resort to that kind of violence?"

Rivera realized that a lot had happened in the two days since he'd last spoken to Dunne, and that he'd failed to keep the BLM Investigative Agent abreast of his progress. It was time to rectify that oversight.

Rivera related to Dunne his conversation with Sheila during which he had learned that a young man was coming to visit Dr. Kennedy, and how Chris Carey had helped him identify the fellow as a former student named Harry Ward. Rivera ran through the story that Ward had told him—about how Kennedy had found a series of shaman petroglyphs which he claimed were all inscribed in the late 1700s by the same man, an old Ute medicine man.

"An *old* Ute?" Dunne smiled with a dubious look on his face. "How did Kennedy know the Ute was old? And for that matter, how did he know the guy was a medicine man?"

"His interest led him to research the Ute oral histories. One of the manuscripts described a special shrine that the Utes visited during the winter solstice. It's a large pile of sandstone rocks in the middle of some sage flats out in the Big Triangle. Turns out that was the site of the first shaman petroglyph." Rivera related the story about the Ute medicine man killing the Spaniard and taking the saddlebags containing the white man's bad medicine, and how the bad medicine had been the cause of many Ute deaths at the hands of Spaniards, and how the medicine man had hidden it in a place far from his people.

The hint of a smile appeared on Dunne's face. "Bad medicine?"

"Gold. To the Utes, it was bad medicine because the Spaniards would kill to get their hands on it." Rivera added the information Van Zandt had given him—about how the Spaniards had converted the raw gold into doubloons. "The saddlebags were full of gold coins."

"And Kennedy found the saddlebags?"

"Right. The series of shaman petroglyphs ended at the cliff dwelling where I found his body. It's within a hundred feet of where Zeke Stanton was shot. I explored the cliff dwelling yesterday. It was a three-room affair, thirty feet up a series of handholds, in an alcove walled in with rocks. I found a depression in the dirt floor of the last room. The depressions looked like they were made by saddlebags."

Dunne thought for a moment. "So whoever killed Dr. Kennedy also made off with the saddlebags full of coins."

"That's the way it looks to me."

Dunne shook his head, still looking confused. "Why didn't Kennedy just take the coins home? Why leave them in the cliff dwelling where someone else might find them?"

"I guess he felt it was safer to leave them where they were. After all, no one had found them for over two centuries. He was quietly selling the coins, one every couple of weeks, to Van Zandt."

"What's the point of selling them one at a time?"

"Van Zandt thought Kennedy wanted to avoid making a big splash and attracting attention, especially from the IRS. The interesting thing is that he kept very little of the money for himself. He donated the bulk of it anonymously to charity."

Dunne sat quietly, staring at the floor, as if digesting the story and testing it for flaws. Finally he nodded. "Okay, so the day Kennedy was killed, he climbed up the handholds to the cliff dwelling, retrieved a coin from the saddlebags to sell to Van Zandt, and climbed back down. Then what? Someone with a pistol was waiting there for him? The killer shoots him and then climbs up to the cliff dwelling to retrieve the coins?"

"Possibly. There's a problem with that, though. Why murder a man if you don't yet know what's stashed up in the dwelling?"

"So whoever shot him already knew about the gold."

"Looks that way." Rivera thought for a long moment. "But that raises another question. If the killer already knew about the gold, why not just go take it when nobody's around. Saves a killing."

"Yeah. It's hard to make sense of it."

"Unless the killer knew Kennedy had found a stash of gold but didn't know where it was. Then he'd have to follow Kennedy to determine the location of the cache."

"Makes sense," said Dunne. "So he follows Kennedy to the cliff dwelling, figures that's where the cache is, waits for him to come down, and shoots him. But he could have hidden and waited for Kennedy to leave. That way, he wouldn't have had to kill him."

"I think that has more to do with the barberry bush that hid the opening in the cliff. The bush was so dense and thick, I couldn't see past it. I had to crawl underneath it to see what was on the other side. I think that when the killer saw Dr. Kennedy crawl under the bush into the opening in the canyon wall, he couldn't have known how far Kennedy was going to go. For all the killer knew, it could have been a slot canyon that went for a quarter mile and opened to a valley somewhere. So the killer had to crawl under the bush to follow Kennedy and then he unexpectedly comes face to face with him."

"But still, why shoot him? Kennedy was pushing fifty. Assuming the killer was younger and stronger, he could have just overpowered him and taken the saddlebags."

"Maybe they knew each other. Maybe the shooter wanted anonymity."

"Yeah. So how does the Zeke Stanton shooting fit into this?"

"I think Zeke was just in the wrong place at the wrong time. Both bullets came from the same gun and both victims had powder burns on their shirts. Zeke must have arrived there just as the killer was leaving. Possibly Zeke challenged him, thinking he might be one of the bighorn poachers. In any case, the killer wanted to eliminate a possible witness, so he shot Zeke."

"By the way, I heard Zeke is doing a little better," said Dunne. "His condition is stable now and the doctor is optimistic, but he still hasn't regained consciousness."

"If he makes it through the ordeal, maybe he can give us a description of the shooter."

Dunne sat quietly for a full minute. "I've been thinking about those saddlebags. It seems to me that, after more than two hundred years, they'd be pretty brittle and cracked by now. The leather would be all dried out. If someone lifted them, the weight of the gold might soon split the bottom open. So maybe the killer had a backpack with him, lifted the saddlebags, and placed them into the backpack. We should add a backpack to the mental picture we've been drawing."

"Good point," said Rivera.

"So what's your next step?"

Rivera laughed. "I have no idea. I guess I'll go back out there, talk to the people at the Center, and revisit the crime scene. I'm sort of at a dead end. The killer could be anyone."

Dunne looked at his watch. "I need to get back to the office." He glanced toward the hallway and lowered his voice. "Before I go, have you heard anything new about the election?"

"No Adam, I've been working. No time for gossip." Rivera smiled. "So what have you heard?"

Dunne laughed. "I thought you said you had no time for gossip."

"Maybe I can squeeze a little in."

"I hear your sheriff is dropping in the polls and the colonel is rising. It's almost a dead heat now."

Rivera nodded noncommittally. "Well, they say not to take polls too seriously." He was reluctant to utter his true feelings about the election as that didn't seem proper, but internally he hoped Campbell would lose. He was fed up with him and ready for a competent boss who cared about more about the citizens of Grand County than a golf game.

Dunne left the office and Rivera resumed his ruminations. He had no likely suspect, but he also had no reason to rule out the residents or staff of the Center, the bighorn poachers, McGinty himself, or even the members of *The Keepers of Order*. For that matter, it could be someone else entirely, though that didn't seem likely.

It had to be somebody who was familiar with that part of the Big Triangle.

He glanced at his watch. It was nearly ten thirty. Gloria had estimated she would pull into Moab around seven o'clock. He wanted to get out to the Big Triangle and back before she arrived. He was eager to see her and hoped she wouldn't be too unhappy when he gave her the news about the sudden increase in his workload. He grabbed his hat and was starting out of his office when Sheriff Campbell darkened his door.

"Where are you going?"

"Back to the Big Triangle to continue my investigation."

"I need for you to come with me to a ladies' club meeting. I'm giving a speech and I want you circulating in the crowd, showing your support. You don't have to say anything. Just be there and pretend you're supporting me."

Rivera could hardly believe his ears. He stood there, staring at Campbell for a long moment. "I can't go with you," he said finally. "I have work to do. There's a killer out in the Big Triangle and I need to stop him before someone else dies."

Campbell frowned and puffed up his chest. "Are you refusing to follow a direct order?" he said in a booming voice, loud enough for most everyone in the building to hear.

Rivera raised his voice. "I've already told you, I can't get involved in the race for sheriff."

"So you're refusing a direct order."

Rivera felt his face flush. He'd reached the limits of his patience. His years of resentment toward Campbell seemed to erupt all at once. His mild-mannered demeanor exploded into anger. He balled up a fist and stepped closer to Campbell. "You're damn right I am."

Campbell stepped back, his face ashen. "Hey, hey, relax, Rivera. There's no need for that. I just wanted to get some help at the ladies' club meeting. That's all. If you don't want to help, fine." He waved a hand dismissively. "Go ahead and do your Big Triangle thing."

Campbell forced a smile, nodded once nervously, and backed out of the office. Rivera stood there, adrenalin pumping through his veins. He looked down at his fist and shook his head. His thoughts reverted to a time in Las Cruces when he was a teenager. His younger sister had come home with a torn dress, crying that an older boy had roughed her up. Rivera sought out the offender and punched him in the face as hard as he could. As a result of the blow, the boy had lost the sight in one of his eyes. Ever since that day, Rivera had sworn to himself he would never again lose his temper and strike another person in anger. Whenever he felt anger rising within him, he worked hard to suppress it. Today, he'd let it get the best of him.

He was embarrassed and disappointed in himself, but maybe that was the only way to communicate with Campbell. The only reason he'd put up with him this long was that he loved his job. Investigative work and solving crimes were the things he enjoyed most about his professional life. Maybe he wouldn't have to put up with Campbell much longer.

# 14

RIVERA BOUGHT A COUPLE of carne guisada tacos and a Dr. Pepper before he left town and ate as he drove. He was still embarrassed at his outburst, but he had to smile at the image of Sheriff Campbell backing down and skulking off to his ladies' club meeting. It was unfortunate the entire staff had to hear his exchange with Campbell. Everyone within earshot had stared at him as he left the building. No one had uttered a word but he thought he'd noticed expressions of approval on their faces. Hopefully, Campbell wouldn't fire him in the morning.

Rivera crossed the Dolores River and continued driving on BLM Route 107 toward the McGinty Ranch. He finished eating the tacos and checked the front of his shirt for gravy stains, relieved to find none. He drank the rest of the soda and stuffed the wrappings and cup into a small garbage bag hanging from the passenger side of his instrument panel. The sight of a clear blue sky and blankets of yellow and purple wild-flowers blooming on the mesa top helped to settle him down. He forced himself to stop dwelling on Campbell's misdeeds and instead concentrate on his case. Now that he understood the motive for the shootings and had a general idea of how they had taken place, he planned more in-depth questioning of McGinty and the residents of the Center for Cosmic Consciousness. He was particularly interested in learning if anyone had been seen following Dr. Kennedy during one of his hikes into the backcountry. He also intended to take another look at the crime scene to see if he had missed anything.

He reached the McGinty Ranch, rumbled across the cattle guard, and drove on the rutted dirt road to the ranch house. Mr. and Mrs. McGinty came out of the house just as he was pulling to a stop. Mrs. McGinty, a small, slender woman with gray hair tied back in a bun, seemed to be impatiently lecturing Mr. McGinty. The wrinkles covering her well-tanned face were made more pronounced by a frown. Rivera got out of his vehicle.

Mr. McGinty, with obvious reluctance, introduced his wife to Rivera.

Rivera touched the brim of his hat. "A pleasure to meet you, ma'am." He turned to Mr. McGinty. "Any sign of the poachers?" he asked.

McGinty produced a nervous laugh and directed his gaze to his feet.

"Tell him, Alvin," said Mrs. McGinty in an exasperated tone of voice.

Mr. McGinty looked embarrassed, said nothing. He shifted his weight to his other foot.

Mrs. McGinty's high-pitched voice rose as she poked a gnarled forefinger in her husband's direction. "You tell him right now, Alvin McGinty. Right this minute, or I will."

"I saw them yesterday morning."

"Why didn't you call me?"

"That Butch Jeffers fella with the militia told me I'd better not. He said if I saw the poachers, I'd better call him and no one else if I knew what was good for me."

"He threatened you?"

"Well, I don't really know if it was a threat—"

"Of course it was a threat, you old fool," said Mrs. McGinty. "Use your head. We're out here alone and that Jeffers boy is an unstable hothead. No tellin' what he's capable of doing."

It was clear to Rivera that Butch Jeffers had intimidated McGinty and his wife. His dislike for Jeffers rose another notch. "You want to press charges? I can have him in jail by morning."

McGinty paused, then slowly shook his head. "He'd be out of jail in no time and we're out here alone, just like the missus said. How about if I call you when I see them, but you don't ever tell anyone where you got the information."

"Fair enough."

"Of course, I'll still have to call Jeffers or he might find out I saw the poachers and didn't tell him. But I'll call you first."

Rivera nodded. "Okay, that's fine."

"If only Alvin Junior had stayed here like I wanted him to," said Mrs. McGinty. "We wouldn't have to worry about that Jeffers." She spun around and started back toward the house, muttering to herself. "But, no, our only child had to go to New York City to make his fortune. On Wall Street instead of here where he belongs. New York City is no place to raise a young family. I told him ..." She was still talking as she climbed the porch steps and entered the house, but Rivera couldn't make out her words.

"Ginny's right about Alvin Junior. We'd be a lot safer if he was here. You couldn't pay me a million dollars to live in New York City. Just look around." He extended his arms in an all-encompassing gesture. "It's beautiful country, isn't it?"

Rivera scanned the landscape. "It sure is." He wished he had more time to admire it. "One last question before I leave. Besides the poachers, have you ever seen anyone else out in that rocky country east of your place?"

McGinty thought. "Not recently. Occasionally some hikers come through here. Haven't seen any in months, though."

As Rivera drove off the ranch, he was fairly certain McGinty could be crossed off the list of suspects—he just wasn't the type. Next stop was the Center for Cosmic Consciousness. He turned left onto the dirt road that led through the rocks and junipers, passed through the front gate, and parked next to the office.

Brother Timothy Pierce opened the door.

"Got a minute to talk?" asked Rivera.

"Sure. Let's go into the living room and sit down," said Pierce, his words slightly slurred.

Rivera detected the smell of alcohol on Pierce's breath. They walked through the office into the living quarters, a deceptively spacious home with some of the finest furnishings Rivera had ever seen. The living room looked like the product of an interior designer's work.

Pierce motioned for Rivera to have a seat on the couch while he sat across from him in an overstuffed chair. "I'm still in shock over Peter's death. What would motivate someone to do a thing like that?"

"That's what I intend to find out." Rivera decided not to mention the gold coins.

"Peter was a bit overbearing at times, but he was a good man. I'll miss him."

"May I ask how long you've lived here?"

"Me? About ten years."

"During that time, have you ever seen or heard of bighorn poachers operating out this way?"

Pierce thought for a moment. Shook his head. "No."

"On the morning Dr. Kennedy disappeared, did you see him leave the Center?"

"No. When he went out on his daily hikes, he didn't leave through the front gate. He went out the back way and headed north from his cabin, directly into that rocky terrain. So I wouldn't have seen him."

"Did any of the others leave the compound on their solo hikes by way of that two track that leads to his cabin?"

"I've never seen that. Usually they leave by the front entrance to find a quiet place to connect with nature. But to be clear, I usually don't pay much attention to which way they leave. It's very possible one or more of them had gone out the back way that day."

Rivera felt mildly disappointed by the answer. The way things stood, his only chance of breaking the case was to identify the individual who had followed Kennedy through the backcountry to the cliff dwelling on the morning he was killed.

"I'm curious about something. May I ask how much you charge people to enroll in your program?"

"Two thousand a month, except for the cabin Dr. Kennedy lived in. Since it's off the grid and pretty minimal compared to the other cabins, I only charge him five hundred a month. I'm not trying to make money here. The rental fees cover my expenses and that's all. Some months, I lose money and I have to make up the difference out of my own pocket. But that's okay, I'm reasonably well off. When I inherited this land from my uncle, I also inherited a significant amount of cash."

Rivera remembered Chris Carey's curiosity about why a Catholic priest would lose his religion, give up the priesthood, and choose to establish the Center. Rivera was curious too. He broached the subject, intending to back off right away if Pierce showed the slightest resentment to an incursion into his private life. "If I'm not getting too personal, would you mind telling me why you established the Center in the first place?"

Pierce looked away, thought for a long moment. "I don't mind, I guess, but it's kind of a long story."

"I have time." He didn't really, but he wanted to hear the story.

Pierce talked about growing up in a devoutly Catholic home in Santa Fe, finishing his degree at St. John's College, and entering the priesthood. He described his early years as a parish priest serving communities in New Mexico and later in Arizona. All went well until he began drinking a little too much to suit his superiors. "I didn't think a few drinks now and then affected my performance as a priest," he said, "but the bishop disagreed. To dissuade my drinking, he transferred me to the Monastery in the Desert, a lonely outpost in New Mexico far away from civilization and alcohol. Of course, the scenery was exquisite, right there on the Chama River, but after a few lonely months of looking at the same view, I didn't even notice it anymore. They sent me there to pray and meditate. I went, of course, and tried praying and meditating all day, every day. After nearly a year, it started to drive me a little crazy. Instead of meditating on the things I was supposed to, I started meditating on the people who had banished me to that wilderness. My resentment grew with each passing month. Who the hell did they think they were?"

Rivera noticed that Pierce was becoming visibly irritated. He was gripping the arms of his chair.

"Nevertheless, I tried to do what they ordered me to do. I read a lot, working my way through a library of religious books. They all said pretty much the same thing. Be a good boy. Do what we tell you to do. Lead your life this way, not that way. It all began to ring a little hollow."

"Is that when you left the priesthood?"

"Not quite. I began to realize that all those books were written by men, just like me. Who's to say what they wrote was correct? In the Vatican, there are rooms full of dusty volumes containing ecclesiastical laws and pronouncements written over the centuries by mere mortals. They purport to dictate how one should lead one's life in order to get to heaven. But Christ's words in the New Testament would occupy no more than a few pages. So where did all those other rules and regulations come from? I realized they were written by men just like the ones who had sent me away. That's when I began having doubts about my religion. I still believed in a higher power, but I began rejecting all

the bureaucratic nonsense dictated by the church lead-
ers. There was a time when it was a sin to eat meat on
Friday, when a woman had to wear a head covering in
church, and when no one but a priest could touch a
consecrated host. Now all that and many other dictates
have been tossed out or changed. Does that mean they
made no sense while they were in effect all those centuries before? It became more and more clear to me
that the laws of the church were all about man-made
rules and not about the wonder of God. When that
realization finally sunk in, I gave up my religion and
left the priesthood."

Rivera had grown up Catholic but had never spent
much time thinking about his religion. He didn't always
obey the laws of the church but tried to live a good life.
He followed a sort of modified Catholicism—don't hurt
anyone, help people whenever you can, go to church
once in a while.

"So what brought you here?" he asked Pierce.

I lost my religion but not my belief in God. I wanted
to get as close to him as I could. I figured the best way
to do that was to sit quietly and admire his accomplishments. Appreciate the things he had done. Look
around at this country, Deputy Rivera. It's a work of art
in whichever direction you look. And on a clear night,
you can see a million stars. Yet there's hardly ever anyone out here to appreciate it. Most people are clustered
together in the cities, fighting traffic, worrying about

overcrowded schedules, hating their jobs, and arguing politics with each other. To me, that makes no sense. It's no way to be happy. As I mentioned to you, I'd inherited this place from an uncle. At first, I lived alone in the cabin where Dr. Kennedy lives ... I mean lived. I loved it and knew I wanted to spend the rest of my life here. But I also wanted some company, and I wanted the people around me to discover for themselves what I had discovered about life. So I set up the program we have here today. I brought in Brother Siddhartha to help the residents find their way to contentment and peace. He is an amazing human being with such a clear-thinking mind. The program is a combination of individual counseling, group discussions, meditation, yoga, and backcountry solo hikes. It doesn't work for everyone, but it gratifies me when the program brings someone to the point where he or she can truly enjoy life. Unfortunately, some people revert to their former lifestyles after leaving here. Those I consider my personal failures."

Rivera smiled. "Interesting story. Thanks for sharing it with me." He looked at his watch. "Do you know if all of the residents are here now?"

"Yes, I believe they are. It's nearly lunchtime."

"Okay, Brother Timothy, thanks for your time. I'll be visiting with each of the residents for the next hour or two."

# 15

RIVERA LEFT BROTHER TIMOTHY and walked to the adjacent cabin which was smaller than Pierce's residence. He knocked on Siddhartha Singh's door and heard a high-pitched voice speaking with a lilt. "Hello. Come in, please."

Rivera pushed open the door and entered. It was a two-room cabin sparsely furnished and minimally decorated. Bookshelves along the far wall were filled to capacity and the air smelled of incense.

Singh was a short, thin man with brown skin. He was wearing a white robe. "Welcome to my home," he said. He smiled, pressed his hands together as if praying, and bowed his head. "I am Siddhartha Singh, at your service."

The interview with Singh was short and sweet. The man was too old and too frail to be involved in either poaching or killing. Rivera doubted he weighed a hundred pounds. If he ever fired a handgun, the recoil would probably knock him over. He had no information of any use and thought Rivera had come to him for counseling. Rivera cut the interview short and beat a hasty retreat.

He consulted his notepad. Harriet Benson, the artist, lived in cabin number two. He walked to her cabin and knocked on the door.

Harriet jerked open the door. She seemed annoyed at the interruption. "Yes? What is it?" she asked in an impatient tone of voice. She was a tall, big-boned woman with brown eyes and blonde hair pulled back in a pony tail. Rivera guessed her age to be about forty. She held a paintbrush in her hand and was wearing a white smock covered with multicolored blotches of paint. Behind her, next to the window, Rivera could see a partially completed oil painting resting on an easel. Of all things, the subject matter was a bighorn ram standing atop a bluff.

Rivera introduced himself and explained the reason for his visit.

She frowned and shook her head. "Boy, you're timing sucks. I'm right in the middle of something here."

"It would only take a couple of minutes." Rivera realized he needed to soften Harriet up if he was going to get information useful to his investigation. He disliked manipulating people but, what the heck, he had a job to do. He craned his neck and looked past the woman, eyes wide open. "That's a beautiful painting."

Harriet's frown disappeared and her voice softened. "Oh, do you think so?"

"It's a very good likeness. I like the way you've got the head tilted upward. Makes the animal look majestic."

She turned and looked back at the painting. "Majestic. Yes. That's exactly the look I was going for. I'm having a little trouble with the face, though. Something doesn't look right but I can't figure out what the problem is. It's very frustrating."

"You made the eyes brown. They should be amber."

She tilted her head and studied the painting. "Yes, I believe you're right. They *should* be amber. Won't you come in?"

"Thank you. I won't stay long." Rivera stepped through the door.

They sat in stuffed chairs in a small living room.

"Nice cabin," said Rivera. "This is the first one I've been inside of." The furnishings were functional and comfortable, but not fancy. There were framed photographs hanging on the walls depicting backcountry scenes. On a small table in the corner were an open book and a vase containing fresh wildflowers. On the far wall was a set of built-in bookshelves filled with books. There was no television or audio equipment.

"Well, to tell you the truth, I wish Brother Timothy had let me bring my own furniture. These furnishings are a little too stark to suit my taste. And he wouldn't allow me to bring my Bose radio and CD collection. I love music but the only kind we get up here is that piped-in flute music in the cafeteria. If you want to know the truth, it sort of drives me nuts. But I suppose if I'm going to benefit from Brother Timothy's program, I'd better obey all the rules."

"How long have you been a resident here?"

"Almost six months."

Rivera couldn't imagine going six months without music. Or even a week. His favorite genres were progressive country, Tejano, certain mariachi songs he learned from his father, and rock and roll music from the seventies and eighties. Flute music was way down on his list.

"Where did you come from?" he asked.

"Santa Fe. I studied at the Santa Fe Art Institute. After my husband left me, I decided to come up here for a change. I like the peace and quiet."

"How well did you know Dr. Kennedy?"

"Not very well. I didn't enjoy being around him much, so I kind of avoided him. He was a little too overbearing to suit my taste. And he introduced himself as *Dr.* Kennedy, not Peter. He was so full of himself. In the cafeteria, I sat as far away from him as I could. Despite the distance, his voice was so loud that I was always victimized by his insufferable lecturing."

"Any idea why someone would want to harm him?"

"Not really. Could have been anyone. No one much cared for him."

"The morning he was killed, did you see anyone following him out into the backcountry?"

"Following him? No, not that I can recall."

"Are you sure?"

She thought for a long moment. "Yes, I'm sure."

"On your own hikes, did you ever see him out there?"

"Yes. One time our paths crossed. I just waved and kept going. I didn't want another lecture."

"Did you see anyone following him on that occasion?"

She shook her head. "No. I'm sure I didn't."

More disappointment. It occurred to Rivera that if none of the residents had seen anyone following Dr. Kennedy on his hikes, he'd be back to square one. He stood up and gave Harriet one of his business cards. "If you remember seeing anything unusual, please give me a call."

On his way out of Harriet's cabin, he saw Bob, the photographer, coming out of his cabin across the driveway. He was holding a suitcase. Rivera consulted the list of residents Brother Timothy had given him and noted that Bob's last name was Livingston. Rivera walked over to him. Livingston was grinning.

"You look happy," said Rivera.

"I am, Deputy. I'm at peace with the world. Yesterday, two of my photographs were accepted for display at the Cenizo Art Gallery in Moab. My first ones ever. I'm ecstatic. The guru has been telling me for weeks to control my desires. Live in the now. He keeps quoting some philosopher named Lao Tse. '*Freedom from desire leads to inner peace,*' or something like that. I say bull, getting two photos accepted at the Cenizo Gallery leads to inner peace." He laughed with glee. "I've learned that I really don't belong here at the Center. I realize now that I do have desires, and working toward fulfilling them is what brings me happiness. I'm leaving here today and moving back to my place in Moab."

Rivera congratulated him and probed him for information on anyone who might have followed Dr. Kennedy during his backcountry hikes. Livingston said he hadn't noticed anyone following him and had little to add to what he had said yesterday. He was happy to be giving up on life at the Center and returning to the real world. It was apparent he was destined to be one of Brother Timothy's failures.

Rivera paid a return visit to Joey Palmer, the former rock star. Once again, when Joey opened the door, marijuana smoke wafted out of his cabin.

"Hey, man, how's it going?"

"Fine. How are you doing?"

"Everything is beautiful."

"Quick question. Have you ever seen anyone following Dr. Kennedy during his hikes out in the backcountry?"

Joey's expression turned grim. "Oh, man, I didn't mean those things I said about him. Last time we talked, I didn't know he was dead. What a bummer. I thought he was just missing. I feel real bad about what I said. I guess he wasn't such a bad guy."

Rivera repeated his question.

Joey thought for a moment. Shook his head. "Nope. Never did." He smiled. "But I'll be looking in on Sheila from time to time, helping her get through the ordeal of losing Kennedy."

Rivera got the impression Joey had more in mind than just helping a grieving woman.

Next on Rivera's list was Claudia Corbett, the poet in the group. He knocked on the door of cabin number eight. A woman with wavy, shoulder-length brown hair answered the door. She looked to be in her early fifties and had large brown eyes and full lips. She was wearing sandals and a flowery, multi-colored shift that looked expensive and completely out of place in the high desert. Her necklace and bracelets, adorned with large imitation gemstones, jangled and rattled with her every movement. She wore gaudy rings on several of her fingers.

She scanned Rivera up and down with a smile and raised eyebrows. "And how may I help you?"

He introduced himself and explained the nature of his visit. "I'd like to ask you a few questions about Dr. Kennedy."

"Of course," she said. "Come inside and get comfortable."

The layout of the cabin was just like Harriet's. He sat in a stuffed chair and Claudia sat directly across from him in a matching chair. She crossed her legs and smoothed her shift over her knee.

"How long have you been a resident here?"

"About three months."

"Where did you come from?"

"Los Angeles, but I had to get away from there. It's so crowded and the freeways are a mess. And the *men*—well, I just got tired of being chased all the time. It's exhausting."

"I'm investigating the murder of Dr. Kennedy and I was wondering what you could tell me about him."

She leaned forward and smiled. "Well, let me tell you. That man lived with his little girlfriend back there in the old cabin. Whenever they came to the cafeteria at mealtime, he was always very attentive to her. He would pull out a chair for her and flatter her and fawn over her, but several times, I mean lots of times, I caught him giving me the once over. That man had a roving eye, I'm telling you."

"Did he ever, you know, make a pass at you or suggest getting together?"

"Well, no, not in so many words, but these are things a woman just knows. She doesn't have to be told. Do you have a woman, Deputy Rivera?"

Rivera had been down this road before. Claudia was in the early stages of coming on to him. "Yes, I do have a woman, but let's get back to Dr. Kennedy. Can you think of anyone who might have wanted to harm him?"

She thought for a long moment. "Maybe that photographer fellow, Bob. I saw him looking at Sheila a time or two. I think he had a thing for her. Maybe he knocked off Kennedy so he could have Sheila."

"But Dr. Kennedy is dead and Bob is leaving the Center today. If he wanted Sheila, wouldn't he be staying?"

"Oh. I didn't know he was leaving." She thought for a moment. "Then what about Joey? I saw *him* looking at her too. You know how those band members were back in the seventies. It was all sex, drugs, and rock and roll. I'd take a good hard look at him if I were you."

"You make the Center for Cosmic Consciousness sound like a little Peyton Place."

"Well, like they say, boys will be boys and girls will be girls."

"When Dr. Kennedy went off on one of his hikes, did you ever notice anyone following him?"

"No. Well, once I saw him headed out the front gate. About a minute later, I saw Theodore headed out the same way."

"When was that?"

"About a month ago, I'd say."

"Anything else you can tell me?"

She smiled. "Only that you're welcome to visit me anytime."

Rivera handed her a business card. "Please call me if you think of anything else.'

She looked at the card, slid it into the top of her shift, and patted it. "I'll be sure to do that."

Rivera thanked her and left. He was smiling. His job brought him into contact with all kinds of people—a cross section of humanity with all its frailties. He checked his notepad. Theodore Atkinson, the newspaper scion, was last on his list. He occupied cabin number four.

Atkinson was a pleasant looking man in his early fifties. He was wearing well-worn jeans, hiking boots, and a faded, plaid shirt with long sleeves. He had a full head of curly, brown hair and was well tanned. He invited Rivera into his cabin and they sat on much the same furniture that Rivera had seen in the other cabins.

"I heard about Dr. Kennedy," said Theodore. "Damn shame. He seemed like a fine fellow."

"Did you know him very well?"

"Not really. About as well as you get to know anyone here at the Center. I saw him during meals and often had discussions with him about his work. I'm from Houston and hadn't seen petroglyphs until I moved out here. I find them fascinating and, of course, Peter knew all about them. Aside from our discussions about petroglyphs, I can't really say I knew him well."

"How long have you been at the Center?"

"Not quite a year."

Rivera repeated the questions he had asked the other residents. "Do you know any reason someone would have wanted to kill him?"

"No."

"Did you ever see anyone following him when he went on one of his hikes into the backcountry?"

"I've never seen anyone following him but I did see him out there the day he was killed."

"Your paths crossed that day?"

"No. I just saw him from a distance. It was about a mile north of the Center, near the place I usually go to for solitude and contemplation. It's up high and has an extraordinary view. Solo hikes into the backcountry are part of Brother Timothy's program here. I was watching three fellows hiking west about a half mile away. Thirty minutes later, I saw Peter hiking. He was also heading west, but on a track about halfway between me and where I saw the three hikers."

Rivera took out his pen and notepad. "The three hikers, can you describe them?"

Theodore laughed. "At a half-mile distant, I couldn't tell much, except that one of them was carrying a rifle. From their movements, I'd guess they were young— maybe in their twenties or thirties. I think I remember that one of them had a beard. They were wearing dark clothing and caps—that's all I can remember."

As Rivera left Theodore's cabin and headed for his vehicle, he realized two things. First, he'd learned nothing that would enable him to rule out anyone at the center as Kennedy's killer, and second, the poachers were operating in the vicinity of where Kennedy was hiking the day he was killed, so he couldn't rule them out either.

Rivera hopped into his pickup and drove to the off-the-grid cabin to visit Sheila. She was in the process of packing up her things.

"I've decided to leave the Center tomorrow. Without Peter, this place has no meaning for me. Staying here would just be heartbreaking."

"Where will you go?"

"I'm going to stay with my mother in Kansas for a while. Maybe someday I'll go back to school and work on my Master's degree."

"Is there anything I can do to help you?"

She thought for a moment. "All of Peter's papers, notes, and photographs are here. I'm going to leave them in the cabin. Would you tell that young man who came to visit Peter that he can have them? Peter said he was interested in petroglyphs, so maybe he can get some use out of them."

"His name is Harry Ward. I'll tell him to stop by and pick up the material after you're gone. I know it will mean a lot to him."

"Thank you."

"One quick question before I leave. When Peter went out on one of his solo hikes, he usually left the cabin and headed directly into the rocks, didn't he?"

"Yes, that's right. He'd go straight back into the rock field that starts behind the cabin."

"Did you ever see anyone following him into the rocks?"

She thought. "Not that I can remember."

After revisiting Gladys and Homer Jones in the Community Center and learning nothing new, Rivera drove out of the Center for Cosmic Consciousness feeling a bit discouraged. The only fact he'd been able to ascertain was that the poachers had been in the area on the same day Dr. Kennedy was killed. He knew he needed a lot more than that if he was going to break the case.

He began thinking about the residents of the Center. Each was dealing with his or her own unique demons. After thinking about that for several minutes, he knew he could never enroll in a program like Brother Timothy's. He had parents and grandparents and friends to help him work through any serious problem he might encounter. Besides, life had too much to offer to waste any of it wallowing in self-discovery.

As he turned onto BLM Route 107, his thoughts turned to Gloria. Was she the one he was destined to spend the rest of his life with? He was almost thirty-eight years old and she had just turned thirty-one. Neither was getting any younger. They'd been dating by long distance for nearly a year. Her home in Abiquiu, New Mexico, was over three hundred miles from Moab, but they'd managed to spend a few days together every two or three weeks. Her elderly parents lived in Española, New Mexico, not far from Abiquiu, and she felt it necessary to look in on them often. And her job was in Rio Arriba County, serving as a deputy sheriff there. So both of them had strong roots in their respective hometowns.

As Rivera approached the turnoff to the two track that led toward the crime scene, he checked his watch. There was still enough time to revisit the scene of the two shootings. He turned right and bumped up the primitive road to its end. He was surprised to see an old, maroon pickup truck parked there. It was a vehicle he didn't recognize. He attempted to run the license plate number but discovered he was in a dead zone where he couldn't make radio or cell phone contact. He parked next to the vehicle, strapped on his daypack, and retraced his steps through the large rocks and foliage toward the crime scene, wary of what might await him there. The trail was overgrown with brush and grasses, so it was rarely used. Yet, only three days after the Stanton and Kennedy shootings, someone had a reason to be there.

# 16

AS RIVERA APPROACHED the opening in the bluff where he'd found Dr. Kennedy's body, a momentary lull in the canyon breeze caused the rustling of the grass and foliage to cease. Through the silence, he thought he'd detected a sound coming from inside the opening. It had sounded vaguely like a grunt. The barberry bush had been trimmed to the ground by the mortuary people, so he had a clear view into the opening. It occurred to Rivera that the scent of Kennedy's blood in the sand might have drawn an animal into the recess, but there was no animal to be seen.

He stepped over the yellow crime scene tape which was now lying on the ground. He'd fastened it about three feet above ground before he left last night. Possibly he hadn't done an adequate job and the night breezes in the canyon had worked it free. Perhaps someone had deliberately torn it loose. He quietly stepped into the opening in the cliff and heard the grunting sound again, louder this time. It came from above, up in the cliff dwelling. He thought for an instant he'd seen a shadow move in the window of the first room. Was it an animal or a human? A bird, maybe? No, it had to be a human—animals don't climb handholds and birds don't grunt.

Rivera drew his Glock and moved closer. He peered into the narrow passageway that led to the hand holds. Now he noticed a few grains of sand falling from above. A leg protruded out from the cliff dwelling, then another, then a torso. The legs dropped downward and moved back and forth, the toes probing for the handholds.

Soon the feet were secure in the handholds and Rivera saw a man emerge from the dwelling and begin descending. He was breathing heavily and there were beads of sweat on his forehead. He glanced downward and spotted Rivera. A smile appeared on his face.

"Howdy, Deputy Rivera," said Harry Ward. When he reached the ground, he shook his head. "I don't know how those cliff dwellers did it. Those handholds are kind of dicey."

Rivera holstered his handgun. "This is a crime scene. What are you doing in here?"

"Well, the tape was down so I thought it would be okay to enter. I wanted to see the cliff dwelling that Dr. Kennedy had found. You wouldn't let me come in here yesterday, so I came back today. Very cool place."

Rivera wasn't sure whether to believe him about the tape. "What were you doing up there?"

"Just exploring. And looking out the windows. I was trying to go back a thousand years in time and imagine what it was like to lead an existence like the Ancestral Puebloan people. All things considered, I prefer my apartment, the internet, and Starbucks coffee. But this dwelling is obviously what that Ute medicine man's shaman figures led to. And from the looks of those depressions in the floor of the last room, I'll bet you found that Spaniard's saddlebags in there, didn't you?"

Rivera smiled. Ward was pretty sharp, just as Chris Carey had reported. Rivera couldn't help liking the young man. "Actually, someone got there before me. I found the depressions too, but no saddlebags."

"Oh. So what do you think was in the saddlebags?" Ward was smiling with an inquisitive expression, as though testing Rivera to see how much he would reveal.

Rivera smiled and shrugged. "I'd guess they were filled with the white man's bad medicine, just like the legend said." There was no way Rivera was going to reveal what he knew about the doubloons. If word got out about the gold, there would be hordes of civilians combing the Big Triangle for the treasure.

"So who do you think made off with the saddlebags?"

"No idea. But whoever took them probably killed Dr. Kennedy in the process."

# 17

MANNY RIVERA COULDN'T take his eyes off of Gloria Valdez. They were sitting at a small table in the corner of Pasta Jay's patio, sipping on glasses of Chianti. Rivera's gaze was focused on her face and everything else in the background seemed to fade into a nondescript fuzziness. To Rivera, Gloria was a classic Hispanic beauty. She was five feet six inches tall and her dark hair fell onto her shoulders, framing her oval face and green eyes. Her lips were full and her smile warmed Rivera's heart. Her skin was smooth and tan and perfect, the only flaw being a tiny scar on the left side of her chin. Rivera had learned the scar was the result of a punch thrown by her abusive husband after he came home from another night of drinking and chasing women. Their brief marriage had ended in divorce years ago and was later annulled in the Catholic Church.

Gloria was wearing tan slacks and a plum colored top, both of which accentuated her shapely figure. She reached over and put a warm hand on his.

"I'm so happy we're together again. I don't like that we live so far apart, but I must say, it does make the times we get together that much more special."

Rivera, who had shed his deputy's uniform and was now wearing pressed blue jeans and a long-sleeve, faded orange shirt, nodded. "I feel the same way. Being with you is the thing I enjoy most in life." It occurred to him to suggest that she stay with him in Moab permanently, but he figured Pasta Jay's patio wasn't the right place to initiate that kind of conversation.

After catching up on all the news in their lives—family, friends, fun, and work—Gloria asked him about his new case.

"It's a real head scratcher."

He spent the next twenty minutes filling her in on the bighorn sheep poaching, the militia called *The Keepers of Order*, the shooting of Zeke Stanton, the McGinty Ranch, the residents at the Center for Cosmic Consciousness, the Ute medicine man legend and how Rivera learned about it, the hike with Harry Ward following the trail of shaman petroglyphs, the discovery of Peter Kennedy's body at the site of the cliff dwelling, the gold doubloon Dr. Pudge Devlin found in Kennedy's pith helmet, and Nick Van Zandt, the buyer of Kennedy's doubloons. Then he put forth his theory that the saddlebags containing Spanish doubloons were what the old Ute meant when he talked about the white man's bad medicine. "I guess the Ute medicine man believed the gold was bad medicine because the Spaniards had killed and enslaved so many of his people as they spread across the Southwest in search of the treasure. I believe whoever killed Dr. Kennedy and shot Zeke Stanton found those saddlebags and made off with the gold."

"So where do you go from here?'

Rivera sighed. "That's the problem. I really don't know. I'll put out the word with coin dealers to see if someone is trying to unload a bunch of doubloons. Other than that, I'm kind of stuck. I don't believe McGinty is involved, and I have no solid reason to believe anyone at the Center for Cosmic Consciousness did it, although I can't rule any of them out, except for Brother Siddhartha. And I can't believe the militia members would shoot one of their own. It could be the poachers, I suppose, but I'm not even sure about that."

They ordered dinner, a fish plate for Gloria and lasagna for Rivera. During the meal, they continued discussing the case. Gloria asked a series of penetrating questions, forcing Rivera to reevaluate and defend his assumptions. She helped him think through the case, step by step from the beginning. She agreed he could rule out McGinty because his life on the ranch with his wife was established and long term. "It's the life he wants, so why risk changing it by killing someone? What would he do with the money? Besides, it would be out of character."

"Exactly my feelings."

"And I don't think the militia people did it because, well, from what you've told me about them, they don't seem bright enough to do the research required to understand that the treasure even existed. The perp had to be pretty smart to pull this off. That leaves the poachers and the people at the Center. If it were the poachers, they're probably gone forever. Why keep poaching bighorns after you've gotten your hands on a fortune in gold coins? I guess I'd concentrate my attention on the people at the Center."

"Makes sense. But it could be someone else altogether."

Rivera appreciated Gloria's help. She had an understanding of murder investigations and showed a sincere and well-informed interest in his work. He liked the way she picked up on the nuances of the case and sized up the players. Her comments reinforced his own feelings. But even so, he still had no idea what the next step in his investigation would be.

After dinner, they walked through town. Moab's Art Walk was in progress this week, and the local art galleries and many of the public spaces had works on display. It was a popular event, and people from all over the region came to Moab to enjoy it. It was a balmy evening, perfect for a leisurely stroll from venue to venue. On display were works from well-known regional artists and unknown locals who showed promise. Gloria loved to visit art galleries and Rivera loved having her on his arm.

Their first stop was the Moab Arts and Recreation Center which was displaying the oil paintings of local, aspiring artists. Most of the paintings featured either backcountry landscape scenes or still life subjects. Gloria spent time chatting with the artists, asking them how they got started, and revealing to Rivera that she'd always had the desire to one day try her hand at oil painting.

They walked to a gallery on Main Street which featured pottery, much of it from artists in the Native American communities of the Southwest. Rivera was attracted to a pair of delicate ceramic bowls crafted by a well-known Hopi artist, but grimaced and backed away when he saw the price tag.

After visiting five separate venues, the couple's last stop was the Cenizo Art Gallery which was featuring American photographers. Rivera signed the guest register for both of them at the entry. Inside, patrons were moving along rows of framed photographs on the walls and speaking in hushed tones. A sound system bathed the room in new age music.

Rivera and Gloria fell in with the crowd, enjoying photographs of the Colorado River at sunset, Monument Valley, the buttes and spires of Canyonlands National Park, the LaSal Mountains at sunrise, a print of Ansel Adam's famous black-and-white photograph titled

*Moonrise,* and a bighorn sheep standing majestically on a rocky bluff. Rivera stopped at the bighorn photograph, noticing the photographer's name was Bob Livingston. He smiled. So this is what Livingston was so excited about. Rivera told Gloria about Livingston and how he'd dropped out of Brother Timothy's program at the Center as soon as he learned that two of his photographs had been accepted for display at the gallery.

They moved to the next photograph. It showed a series of handholds leading up a red-rock cliff face. Rivera was startled by the image and stepped in for a closer inspection. It looked exactly like the steps leading to the cliff dwelling he'd found behind the barberry bush. The photographer was Bob Livingston.

Rivera glanced over his shoulder to make sure no one besides Gloria was within earshot. He turned to her and lowered his voice to a whisper. "Gloria, look at that photograph. Those look like the handholds I climbed yesterday to get into the cliff dwelling I told you about. That's the place where I found Peter Kennedy's body."

"I've seen a lot of those ancient handholds in the New Mexico backcountry. Don't they all look pretty much the same?"

"The pattern and shape of the handholds look very familiar." He pointed. "Look at that third handhold from the bottom—it has kind of a triangular shape. I remember that. And that clump of grama grass growing out of that crack in the rock looks familiar."

"Why is that significant? He might have gone there and taken the photographs after you left the crime scene. Sometimes morbid curiosity causes people to duck under the crime scene tape and take a look around."

Rivera stood staring for a long moment. "What's got my interest is more than just the handholds and the grama grass. Look at the sandy bottom in that narrow passageway. You can see two different sets of footprints—two going in and two coming out. Those are the same prints I saw when I got there."

"But couldn't he have taken the photo after you left?"

Rivera extracted his cell phone and clicked through the photos he'd taken at the crime scene, two of which showed the footprints clearly. He showed them to Gloria. "This image is pretty small, but take a look. What's missing from the photograph here in the gallery are *my* footprints. After I discovered Kennedy's body, I entered the passageway and climbed up the handholds into the cliff dwelling. If Livingston took this photograph after I left the scene, my prints would be there as well."

"So he must have been there before you."

"Right." Rivera escorted Gloria away from the crowd. "I can't believe it. Livingston seemed like such a nice guy. An aspiring artist. Now it looks like he's the killer. If I've got the sequence right, he must have followed

Dr. Kennedy to the cliff dwelling. Kennedy climbed up to the rooms to retrieve one of the doubloons. Then he climbed back down. When he got to ground level, Livingston shot him. Then Livingston climbed up the handholds, loaded the saddlebags into a backpack, and climbed down. He crawled under the bushes, probably pushing his backpack ahead of him. Then he stood up, strapped on the backpack, and walked about a hundred feet where he unexpectedly encountered Zeke Stanton. Wanting no witnesses to the crime, he shot Zeke and left."

Rivera spoke with Sylvia, the owner of the gallery. A forty-something blonde, she wore five-inch heels and a dress unusually stylish for Moab. He'd known her ever since she'd moved to Moab three years ago and opened the gallery.

"Sylvia, I was just looking at the photographs taken by Bob Livingston. He lives here in Moab, doesn't he?"

"Yes, he does."

"I'd like to talk to him. Do you have his address?"

"Sure, Manny. Let me get it for you." She retrieved an index card from a small box on her desk and read off Livingston's address which Rivera jotted in his notepad. "Too bad you didn't come earlier. Bob was here for a few hours, schmoozing with the patrons. He left about an hour and a half ago. Are you interested in buying one of his photographs?"

"Not really. I just wanted to ask him a couple of questions."

"Just between you and me, Bob tries hard but he doesn't seem to have the kind of talent needed to break through to the next level. He's been pestering me for a year to display some of his work. I told him yesterday that I had some open space on the wall for the Art Walk and invited him to display a couple of his photographs. He jumped at the chance. Did you know he also fancies himself as a sculptor?"

"No I didn't. Is he any good?"

Sylvia looked over her shoulder, leaned into Rivera, and covered her mouth with her hand. "Not good at all," she whispered, suppressing a giggle.

Rivera and Gloria walked back to his Sheriff's Department pickup truck. He was feeling pangs of guilt about working on his case while Gloria was visiting instead of giving her his full attention. He would have to find a way to make it up to her.

# 18

A CRESCENT MOON rose over the LaSal Mountains and Venus hung brightly over the Moab Rim as Rivera drove his pickup to Livingston's address. The home, a two-story, white clapboard structure just south of the city limits, was located next to a former gas station which its owner had converted into a bar and grill called Augie's. Augie's had an outdoor patio where a local band was now playing David Bowie's *Fame*. The patio was crowded with patrons dancing, drinking, and laughing.

Rivera turned into the driveway and parked. He removed his handgun from the glove compartment and strapped it on. He hung his badge wallet on his shirt pocket, exited the vehicle, and began moving toward the house. Gloria followed along behind him in the darkness.

"Be careful, Manny."

Rivera stopped and looked at her. His protective instincts took over. "Maybe you should wait in the truck."

She pulled a handgun out of her purse and checked the load. "No way. I'm your backup. Now that I've found you, I'm not going to let anything happen to you."

Rivera smiled. He walked to the door and knocked with his left hand, his right hand resting on the hilt of his gun.

An overweight man in his fifties wearing baggy shorts and a stained undershirt opened the door. He looked at Rivera with a frown. "Can I help you?"

Rivera heard a television blaring in the background. It sounded like an old western movie with horses galloping and guns blazing. "I'm looking for Bob Livingston. Does he live here?"

The man cupped a hand behind his ear. "What? I can't hear you with all that damn music coming from Augie's. I don't know why they have to play so loud."

Rivera raised his voice. "I'm looking for Bob Livingston. Does he live here?"

The man jerked a thumb over his shoulder. "Bob rents the trailer in back. Just continue down the driveway to the creek. It's just beyond a big desert willow."

Rivera headed down the gravel driveway toward the trailer, Gloria walking next to him. The trailer was constructed of sheet aluminum and appeared old and decrepit. Its wheels had been removed and the unit was resting on stacked cinder blocks. It was about thirty feet long and looked like it had been sitting in the same spot for decades. There were two windows and a door on the side from which the deputies approached. Light shone through the windows, both of which had been duct taped around the edges, presumably to keep the cold air from leaking through the seams. Two rusted wrought iron chairs and a small table rested under the desert willow. Wooden steps led up to the door.

Rivera walked up the steps of the trailer, Gloria keeping to his left, her eyes fixed on the windows. He started to knock on the door, then noticed it was ajar. "Hello?" he said in a loud voice. "Hello?"

There was no response. He drew his weapon and pushed the door with his foot. Inside, he saw a man lying face up on the floor, his eyes still open. Rivera shoved the door all the way open and entered the trailer. He scanned the interior and saw no one else. Gloria climbed the steps and followed him inside.

"Is he dead?" she asked.

Rivera dropped to one knee, pressed his forefinger against the victim's neck, and felt for a pulse. He nodded. "He's dead. Looks like a gunshot wound to the chest."

"Is that Bob Livingston?"

"Yes, it is." Rivera stood up, shook his head, and called the dispatcher. He reported the matter and requested the Medical Examiner be sent immediately.

"This case gets stranger and stranger," he said. "After I saw that photograph of the handholds in the gallery, I was sure Livingston was our man. Now I don't know what to think."

During the following two hours, Dr. Pudge Devlin arrived and pronounced Livingston dead, and the mortuary people carted Livingston's body off to the autopsy room at the Moab Regional Hospital. Now it was nearly midnight, and Rivera and Gloria remained to see what they could learn about Livingston. They slipped on latex gloves and began a search of the trailer.

The light inside was less than optimal. The bulbs in the fixtures were all sixty watts or less. Flashlights helped some but they created annoying shadows. There was no substitute for daylight.

The first thing Rivera noticed was an open numismatic catalogue sitting on a small table under a gooseneck lamp. Next to it was a rectangular, hand-held magnifying glass and two rusted, iron cylinders about an inch in diameter and four inches long. As he was inspecting the cylinders, he noticed a coin which had been shielded from view by the catalogue. He sat down in a small chair next to the table, turned on the lamp, and inspected the coin. It looked exactly like the doubloon Pudge Devlin had found in Dr. Kennedy's pith helmet. Now there was no question in Rivera's mind that Livingston was the one who had taken the saddlebags.

Livingston's numismatic catalogue was similar to the one Van Zandt had used. It was opened to a page which displayed an image matching the coin on the table. The coin's wholesale value at was listed at $4,400. Rivera showed the coin to Gloria and pointed his finger at the value listed in the catalog.

"Good Lord," she said. "If those saddlebags were full of coins like this one, can you imagine what the total value would be?"

Rivera thought, nodded. "Well into the millions, I'm sure. More than enough motive for murder." Rivera inspected the cylinders. "Look at these." He handed one to Gloria. "These are the dies Nick Van Zandt told me about. They were used by the Spaniards to make impressions on blank gold disks, turning them into official Spanish coins. This cylinder is for one side of the coin, and the one you're holding is for the other side. I'll have to ask Van Zandt what he can tell me about them. Rivera placed the cylinders and the coin in three separate evidence bags.

He made a search of Livingston's trailer. There was no sign of the saddlebags or a backpack that might have been used to carry the saddlebags. He suppressed a yawn. "Maybe we have a scenario that goes something like this. Livingston follows Dr. Kennedy to the cave, kills him, and removes the saddlebags from the cliff dwelling. He loads the saddlebags into a backpack and leaves. On the way out, he shoots Zeke Stanton to eliminate a witness. Livingston comes home, zips open the backpack and, curious about the value of the coins, he removes one and checks its value in the numismatic catalogue. That explains the coin on the table. Livingston learns yesterday that two of his photos have been accepted for display at the gallery. This afternoon he visits the gallery to promote his work. Then he returns home. Afterwards, someone else enters the trailer, shoots Livingston, and takes the backpack. The shooter is in a hurry to get out of there and doesn't notice the coin on the table. No one hears the gunshot because of the loud music next door."

Gloria thought about that for a moment. "Probably, but that presupposes one thing. The killer had to know Livingston had the coins in his possession. It's not likely this was a random break in. Who would choose an old trailer like this for a robbery instead of a more upscale home?"

Rivera stifled a yawn. "Right. Good point. Someone must have learned about Livingston's windfall between the time he took it from the cliff dwelling and the time he was killed."

"Or maybe knew about it all along. I wonder if Livingston walked in while the killer was here."

Rivera inspected the door. "It doesn't look like the door was forced, so I'd bet the killer arrived *after* Livingston returned home from the exhibit. Maybe the killer knocked on the door and when Livingston opened it, he was staring at a gun."

Gloria reflected on that. "Unless the killer had a key. The landlord must certainly have one. Maybe others do as well."

"But, if that's the case, why wait for him to come home? Why not just take the coins and run?" he asked, talking through a yawn. "There are still lots of unanswered questions, but it's getting late and I'm tired. I'll bet you are too. Let's get out of here. I can come back in the morning and look through the trailer in the daylight.

They strung crime scene tape around the trailer, hopped into the pickup, and drove to Rivera's home.

# 19

RIVERA AWAKENED TO the sound of Gloria humming in the kitchen and the smell of breakfast cooking on the stove. He rolled out of bed and padded into the kitchen in his shorts. Gloria was cooking hash browns, eggs, and sausage, his favorite breakfast. She was wearing snug jeans and a flowery blouse. He walked up behind her, put his arms around her, nuzzled her neck, and inhaled her fragrance. She set the spatula down and leaned back into his embrace. Her cheeks expanded into a smile.

"Are you hungry this morning?" she asked.

"I'm always hungry."

"I looked but I couldn't find any fruit or yogurt or bran flakes in the house."

"Yeah. I'll have to stock up on that stuff someday. Start eating right."

She laughed. "You don't sound very convincing."

"I know. I'm not sure I could survive the transition to health food. My body would probably go into shock."

He picked up a container of tropical fish food and started to feed the guppies.

"I've already fed them. Bentley too. He's out in the yard."

Rivera smiled. He wasn't used to having someone help him with his chores around the house. It was a pleasant change from his bachelor life. "Thank you," he said.

And now it was time to break the unpleasant news to Gloria that he would have to continue working during her visit. "Gloria, I'm real sorry about the timing of these murders. I'd planned some day hikes for us but, as it turns out, I need to keep working. I've got to go to Monticello this morning and get Nick Van Zandt's take on those cylinders we found in Livingston's trailer. Then I need to return to the trailer and see if I can find a lead on who might have killed Livingston."

"Oh, I knew our plans had to change as soon as you told me at Pasta Jay's about Zeke Stanton and Dr. Kennedy. I've seen you before when you're involved in a case—you don't let up until it's solved. It's okay, as long as I get to spend the day working with you."

*Why not*, thought Rivera. She's a trained deputy. And he could use some help. Besides, he loved spending time with her. "I'd like that," he said.

As Rivera pulled up to the curb in front of the sheriff's building, he reminded Gloria about Sheriff

Campbell's unpleasant demeanor. "Be forewarned," he said. "He's rude beyond belief."

Although Gloria had visited Rivera in Moab several times before, this was the first time he'd taken her to the office. He made the introductions to the staff members in the lobby area and told Millie Ives, the dispatcher, that Gloria would be assisting him in his investigation. Then he escorted Gloria to his office and closed the door.

On his desk were two messages. He read the one from Adam Dunne first. It said Zeke Stanton had regained consciousness and was doing much better. His health was improving and his vital signs were approaching normal. He had been moved by ambulance from Grand Junction to the Moab Regional Hospital last night at the request of his family.

The second message was from Dr. Pudge Devlin with the preliminary results of Livingston's autopsy. It confirmed what Rivera already knew. Livingston was killed by a single shot to the chest. Devlin said he would bring the bullet to Rivera's office later this morning.

Rivera looked at Gloria. "We just caught a break. Zeke Stanton is conscious and recovering in the Moab hospital. Now we can get an eyewitness report on the shooting. We'll visit him before we drive down to Monticello."

Just then, there was a gentle knock on the door. The door was opened and a smiling Sheriff Denny Campbell walked in. His manner was polite and even courtly.

"Good morning, Manny. I heard your friend Gloria was visiting and I just wanted to stop by, meet her, and say hello."

Rivera almost didn't recognize this mild-mannered version of his boss. He stood up and made the introductions.

Campbell bowed his head slightly. "It's a great pleasure to meet you, Gloria."

Gloria seemed taken aback. "An honor to meet you, sir. I've heard a lot about you."

Campbell laughed. "Well, don't believe everything Manny says about me. How long are you in town for?"

"Just a couple of days."

"I heard you're helping Manny with his case."

"Just tagging along. Maybe I can learn something about detective work."

Rivera was baffled by the conversation. He'd never seen Campbell so polite. And Campbell never referred to him as *Manny*.

"I read Manny's report on that case you two solved down in Rio Arriba County," said Campbell. "I'd say you already know quite a lot about detective work."

"Well, sometimes it helps to have someone to bounce ideas off of."

"Very true. Can I get you a cup of coffee?"

"No thanks, Sheriff. I just had a cup."

"Very well then, I'll leave you two alone. It was a pleasure meeting you, Gloria." Campbell shook her hand and closed the door quietly as he left.

Gloria turned to Rivera with an astonished look on her face. She spoke in a whisper. "I thought you said he was mean. He seems like a real gentleman to me."

Rivera sighed. Campbell had to pick this one time to be civil, just when Gloria was visiting. Now all the stories Rivera had told her about his overbearing boss would be called into question. Either Campbell was faking it in order to get Rivera to help him with his campaign, or he was so taken by Gloria's attractiveness that he fell out of character. "I've never seen him like this before. This is a rare moment."

"Why, he's absolutely charming. You should give him another chance."

Rivera slowly shook his head. "You know, he must have figured I'd told you a lot of negative things about him. So this play acting was payback for my not helping him with his reelection campaign. I think he was just trying to make me look bad."

Gloria laughed. "Do you really think he's that devious?"

"I do now."

Rivera and Gloria drove to the Moab Regional Hospital and located Zeke Stanton's room. Stanton was awake but appeared groggy and tired. He had a tube running into his nose and an IV in his left arm. He looked uncomfortable. The attending nurse had instructed the deputies to stay no longer than a couple of minutes.

Rivera introduced himself and Gloria. "I'm glad you're doing better. Do you feel up to answering a couple of questions?"

Stanton nodded gingerly.

"I'm going to show you a photograph of a man and I'd like you to tell me if he was the one who shot you." Rivera reached into his shirt pocket and extracted a photo of Bob Livingston.

"I don't need to see a photograph. I know who shot me. It was Bob Livingston. We know each other from the Sierra Club hikes."

Rivera showed him the photograph, just to be sure.

"Yeah, that's him."

"Can you tell me what happened?"

"I was part of a group looking for those guys who were poaching bighorn rams. I was walking through a small canyon when I heard a bush rustling by the canyon wall. I turned and saw a red backpack being pushed out from underneath the bush. I watched until a man emerged and stood up. It was Livingston. He didn't see me at first. He dusted himself off and put on the backpack. Then he noticed me standing there watching him. He walked toward me, smiled, and said,

'Hey Zeke, what are you doing out here?' I started to answer. Then he pulled out a pistol, pointed it at me, and fired. I felt an awful pain in my chest. He walked away and left me there. I guess he assumed I was dead. I managed to call James Kirtland for help, and then I guess I must have blacked out."

"Before you saw Livingston, did you hear an earlier gunshot?"

Stanton thought for a moment. "As a matter of fact, I did—a few minutes before I saw Livingston. I had just entered the mouth of the canyon. I thought it might have been the poachers, so I called the others and then moved up the canyon toward where the sound came from. I remember wondering if the poachers had just killed another bighorn."

"You're lucky to be alive."

"I hope you're going to arrest Livingston."

"Livingston is dead. It's a long story."

Stanton looked relieved. "I can't say I'm sorry."

"Okay, Zeke. We'll leave you alone now to get some rest. Thanks for the information."

As Rivera and Gloria left Stanton's room, they saw three men sitting in the hallway. The Jeffers brothers and James Kirtland had come to visit their fellow militia member. Butch Jeffers gave Rivera a threatening look as he approached. Rivera stopped in front of the group and pointed toward Stanton's room. "That's the kind of thing that happens when amateurs try to enforce the law."

Butch stood up. "We're going back out there again, and there's nothing you can do to stop us."

"It's not against the law to go looking for them," said Rivera, "but if you shoot someone, you'll probably end up in prison for a long time." He looked at Butch's two companions and jerked his thumb toward Butch. "This guy is going to get you in real trouble. He's not the kind of leader you want to be following." Rivera turned and started down the hallway, Gloria at his side.

"Pretty lady," said Butch in a sing song, taunting tone. He tilted his chin up and assumed a tough-guy stance, as though ready to fight.

Rivera walked back to him. The expression on Butch's face transitioned from macho and challenging to hesitant and apprehensive. Rivera smiled. "You want me to face plant you again?"

Butch took a couple of steps back. "I'm telling my uncle about this. This is the second time you harassed me. I'll have you fired."

Rivera looked at Butch's two companions. "Impressive, isn't he?" He turned and left.

Rivera and Gloria walked down the hallway and turned the corner. "I'm not trying to be mean," said Rivera by way of explanation. "I just don't want to see those two young men get into trouble. They're gullible and naive. They need to see Butch not as their fearless leader, but as a coward and a fool."

As Rivera drove south out of Moab toward Monticello, he glanced out the driver's side window. "Look at that sky," he said to Gloria.

The sun was peeking over the snow-capped LaSal Mountains now, backlighting the wispy cirrus clouds that hung high in a blue sky. They were shaped like long feathers and glowed a pink-orange color.

She peered past Rivera, looking at the sunrise. "It is beautiful. I can see why you fell in love with this part of the country."

Rivera wanted to ask her how she would feel about living in Moab but decided to leave that conversation for another time. He was beginning to get mental images of the two of them married, living together, and raising a family. A son and daughter were part of the picture—maybe one of each wouldn't be enough.

They arrived in Monticello and parked in front of the Van Zandt home. Van Zandt pulled the door open even before they rang the doorbell.

"I saw you pulling up. Ever since I received your phone call, I've been looking out the window. I was so looking forward to seeing those cylinders you'd found. Come in, please."

Rivera made the introductions and they sat down in the living room. Rivera handed Van Zandt the coin and the cylinders he'd found in Livingston's trailer.

Van Zandt's face lit up as he studied the cylinders. "Ah, these are some of the dies I told you about. They are quite rare. Worth a lot of money. This is what the Spaniards used to imprint the doubloons." He turned to Gloria. Apparently for her benefit, Van Zandt repeated what he'd already told Rivera about the coin minting process. "They would heat the gold, hammer it out into flat sheets, and cut circular blanks from the sheets. They would hammer these dies onto the gold blanks to imprint the coins. Then they would trim them to the correct weight. That way, they could produce official Spanish currency here in the New World." He returned his attention to Rivera. "This is a very exciting find—let me get my magnifying glass."

He got up and returned, magnifying glass in hand. He inspected the coin first and then the dies. "All dies are slightly different. They have slight flaws or irregularities since each was handmade, one die at a time." He compared the coin to one of the dies. "Ah, yes. This coin was definitely produced using this die. You can see a tiny notch on the right arm of the cross." He held the die and the coin out for Rivera and Gloria to inspect. "See? The die has that same flaw."

Rivera looked closely and nodded. "Yes, I see what you mean."

Van Zandt turned the coin over and compared it to the other die. "Yes. Definitely. The Hapsburg shield has a couple of flaws in the die which correspond to marks on the coin. If I might ask, where did you find these dies?"

"At a private residence in Moab. It was a crime scene. Another murder took place last night."

"And the coin you showed me yesterday was found out in the Big Triangle?"

"That's right. At a different crime scene."

"Very interesting. Let me check something." He retrieved the photographs he'd taken of the first coin and compared the two coins. "Both coins were produced using these dies. They have the exact same flaws."

That confirmed what Rivera had already surmised. Both coins were from the saddlebags the old Ute medicine man had carried to the cliff dwelling. What had been conjecture had just become a certainty.

"Do you still have some of the coins you bought from Dr. Kennedy?" asked Gloria.

"Great idea," said Rivera. "Let's see if they were all made using these dies."

Van Zandt shifted in his seat, appearing uncomfortable. "Regretfully, all of those coins have been sold," he said.

Rivera realized instantly that Van Zandt would have said that whether or not he'd actually sold the coins. He was probably worried that if the feds learned of their existence, they might one day come and confiscate them. Or tax them. Rivera pictured Van Zandt's coins safely stored away where federal or state eyes would never behold them.

"But I do have photographs of them," said Van Zandt. He stood up and extracted a photo album from a bookshelf. He lowered himself back into his seat with a loud wheeze and opened the album. "I kept photographs of every doubloon Dr. Kennedy sold me. Let me check them." Using his magnifying glass, he scanned over a dozen pages of photographs, four mounted on each page. He took his time studying them, and each time he turned a page, he seemed to smile and shake his head, as if in wonderment. Finally he looked up. "My word. I can't believe it. All the coins Kennedy sold me have the exact same flaws as your two coins. I had no reason to check for flaws at the time, so I didn't notice the similarity. This means all of Kennedy's coins and the two you brought me were made from these dies."

"Did Dr. Kennedy tell you the story of the old Ute medicine man and how his petroglyphs led to a remote cliff dwelling where the coins were hidden?"

"No, he didn't, but you have my undivided attention."

Rivera told Van Zandt the whole story while the collector listened with rapt attention.

"What a marvelous story. A provenance like that adds value to the coins—collectors of old coins rarely know the route a coin takes as it travels from its birth at minting to the time when it rests in the collector's hand. With these coins, one has that information. How wonderful. You know what I think, Deputy? I think that saddlebag full of coins had been freshly minted and that horseman was delivering them to some destination where they would be put into circulation. When the time is right, I'd like to make a bid on the two coins and the dies. Collecting old things of value is my life. Please keep me in mind."

"I definitely will."

# 20

RIVERA EASED HIS PICKUP down the long driveway that led to Livingston's trailer and parked next to the desert willow.

"Let's see what things look like in the daylight," he said to Gloria. "We need to make a thorough search of the trailer and learn as much as we can about Livingston. The more we know about him, the better chance we have of identifying his killer."

"Okay. Why don't I start on the outside?" she said. "There's a small trash barrel out there I'll go through. I'll also take a look around for footprints although the ground here is mostly gravel so it probably won't show much."

"Thanks. I'll take the inside." Rivera climbed the steps, opened the door, and made a cursory inspection of the trailer. The front part of the trailer housed a kitchen area with a small refrigerator and an electric range with two coil elements. In the rear was a small bedroom with a double bed, a narrow clothes closet, and a built-in dresser with four drawers.

The center part of the trailer was living space with a worn couch and an adjacent bookshelf. Across from the couch was an older model television mounted high on the wall. Below the TV was a long table cluttered with photographic equipment on one end. On the other end was a sculpture which had been constructed by soldering nuts, bolts, and washers together. Rivera stared at it. It seemed to be a bear standing on its hind legs but he couldn't be sure. Below the table were dozens of clear plastic sacks from the hardware store filled with nuts, bolts, and washers—the raw materials for Livingston's sculptures.

The photographic equipment consisted largely of a digital camera, a computer, an expensive-looking color printer, and several packages of high quality photographic paper. Several photographs cropped in different ways were stacked next to the printer. They were various versions of the same images Rivera has seen at the gallery. On several of the cropped-off photo fragments, he could just make out the edge of Dr. Kennedy's pith helmet. Under the table was a collection of colorful rocks common to the canyon country. Livingston had accumulated about a hundred of them. Rivera inspected the contents of a trash can and found empty plastic sacks from the hardware store and the wrappers of a couple of Snickers candy bars.

He walked into the kitchen and checked the contents of the drawers under the counter top. In the bottom drawer, he found two boxes of .38 caliber cartridges, one full and the other partially full.

Gloria entered the trailer as Rivera was inspecting the drawers in the bedroom. "Find anything interesting?" she asked.

"I found some .38 caliber ammo in the kitchen. Not much else."

"Isn't that the same caliber of the bullets extracted from Zeke Stanton and Dr. Kennedy?"

"Yes, it is."

"Any sign of a handgun?"

"No. He probably ditched it after he shot Kennedy and Stanton. It's probably buried somewhere out in the Big Triangle."

"Makes sense."

"I found some photographic prints of the place where Dr. Kennedy was killed. On some of the cropped-off pieces, you can see the edge of Kennedy's pith helmet."

Gloria looked at the sculpture and smiled. "I noticed that thing last night. What in the world is it supposed to be? A dog begging for food?"

Rivera laughed. "I thought it was a bear or maybe a gorilla standing on its hind legs."

"Oh, well. I'm sure he had something in mind. At least he tried."

"Did you find anything outside?"

"I went through the trash barrel. Nothing useful. Just some banana peels, old newspapers, and candy wrappers. I found some unusual imprints in the ground in places where there was more dirt than gravel. Nothing I could recognize. The edge of a footprint maybe, a couple of gashes that could be anything, a bull's-eye pattern in a couple of places, a star-like pattern, and some paw prints. Maybe a dog or a coyote. I looked for tire imprints but couldn't find any. I've got photos of everything." She handed Rivera her camera.

He stepped through the pictures and studied each image. Shrugged. "None of these rings a bell with me. Let's look at what's stored in Livingston's camera and computer."

Rivera studied the images stored in the camera while Gloria reviewed the computer files.

"A lot of these photographs were taken out in the Big Triangle," said Rivera. "I recognize some of the rock formations from the canyon where the Center for Cosmic Consciousness is located. There are lots of photos of animals taken with a telephoto lens. Most are shots of bighorn sheep."

"Are you thinking Livingston was out there as a spotter for the poachers?'

"That possibility crossed my mind, but the poaching has been going on for a year and Livingston had been living at the Center for only a month."

"There are lots of images stored in his computer too," said Gloria. "All of them look like backcountry shots. I noticed that none of them involve people. I wonder if maybe Livingston didn't have friends."

"Probably a loner. He seems like a fellow who wanted to become a successful artist, either in photography or sculpture, but wasn't blessed with a great deal of talent."

After an hour of searching, they'd found nothing more of interest. No saddlebags and no sign of the red backpack Zeke Stanton had mentioned.

Just before leaving, Rivera decided to peruse the books on Livingston's bookshelf. They were all novels—Tony Hillerman, Scott Momaday, John Nichols, and Rudolfo Anaya—except for a University of New Mexico yearbook. Rivera opened it, thumbed through the section containing the Arts and Science graduates, and found Livingston's picture. His face had a neutral, almost somber cast. Below the picture was his name and nothing more, whereas most of the other graduates had their extracurricular activities listed below their photographs. Evidently, Livingston had participated in none. Remembering that Dr. Kennedy had taught at the university, Rivera flipped through the pages until he came to the faculty section. Kennedy was listed as an associate professor of anthropology. The paragraph below his picture included his professional credentials and noted that he was voted by the student body as the most popular teacher at the university.

Rivera considered that. Certainly he was popular with a certain coed by the name of Sheila Nelson. He flipped through the pages and found Sheila's photograph. She looked young and pretty and had a winning smile. She listed more extracurricular activities than most, and must have been popular because she had been voted vice-president of her sorority. She'd also been active in the Drama Club, the Homecoming Committee, and the Chess Club. Rivera turned to the section on the Drama Club and found a picture of Sheila in costume, playing Desdemona in an Othello play.

Rivera shared the information with Gloria and closed the book. "Poor girl. She went from being on top all the way to the bottom," he said.

"She's young. She's got plenty of time to get her life back on track."

They locked up the trailer and began the drive back to Rivera's office.

"Let's review what we know," said Rivera. "Bob Livingston somehow learns that Dr. Kennedy has discovered a cache of gold coins."

"Wait. Maybe he didn't know it was gold coins," said Gloria. "Maybe all he knew was that it was something of value."

"Right. So he moves to the Center of Cosmic Consciousness to get closer to Kennedy so he can follow him each day on his hikes. One day, Livingston follows him to the cliff dwelling, kills him, puts the saddlebags into his red backpack, and leaves. On the way out, he runs into Zeke Stanton and shoots him. Then he goes home, removes a single coin and the two dies from the saddlebags, and checks the coin's value in the numismatic catalogue. Three days later, he notifies Brother Timothy he's leaving the Center. That evening, he goes to the gallery to mix with the patrons and answer any questions they had about his photographs. Then he goes home. It's dark. Someone knocks on his door, the door opens, and a pistol is pointed at him. He steps back, takes a bullet to the chest, and dies. The red backpack is taken by the killer."

"And no one hears the gunshot because of the loud music coming from Augie's."

"Right. But there are still two perplexing parts to the story. First, how did Livingston learn that Dr. Kennedy had found something of value? I mean, why did he move to the Center and begin following Dr. Kennedy in the first place? And second, how did Livingston's killer learn that Livingston had come into possession of this thing of value? Killing Livingston wasn't done by some burglar that just happened along. It took fore-knowledge and planning."

"I wouldn't be surprised if the answers to those two questions were intertwined somehow," said Gloria. "But focusing for the moment on the second question, it seems the killer would have to be someone who knew Livingston."

"That would include all of his acquaintances in Moab and everyone at the Center for Cosmic Consciousness. And probably others."

"And we should probably add Nick Van Zandt's name to the list of possibilities," said Gloria. "He's smart enough and, although he's probably not physically capable of doing it himself, he might have had an accomplice."

"Right. And add Harry Ward's name to the list too. He's got the mind to figure it out and he's an expert on Dr. Kennedy's work. He wasn't in Moab when Dr. Kennedy was killed, but he's here now, so he had the opportunity to kill Livingston. I like the kid and I don't think he's capable of murder, but I can't rule him out. In fact, let's see if Ward is at his motel right now. Maybe he can account for his time last night and we'll be able to scratch his name off the list."

Rivera turned into the parking lot of the Ramada Inn. On the way to Ward's room, he spotted the young man lying in a lounge chair by the swimming pool, basking in the sun. Ward smiled and waved when he saw Rivera.

"Hi, Manny. Oops. Is it okay if I call you Manny? I feel like we're friends since we went on a hike together."

"Sure, Harry. Manny's fine." Rivera sat down on an adjacent chair.

"Guess what I've decided to do." There was excitement in Ward's voice. "Dr. Kennedy's girlfriend Sheila is moving out of the cabin at the Center for Cosmic Consciousness and going back to her hometown, so I'm going to move into the cabin and live there. I aim to keep my promise to Dr. Kennedy and continue his research into Fremont and Ute petroglyphs. That will be my dissertation topic when I enroll in the PhD program at the University of New Mexico. What do you think?"

"Well, I think it's a fine idea."

"I plan to move out there first thing in the morning."

"Listen, I need to ask you a few questions about your activities yesterday. Can you account for your time between four o'clock in the afternoon and nine o'clock at night?"

"Is this about that Livingston guy who got killed? I heard about it on the news."

"That's right."

Ward thought for a long moment. "Um. I had dinner at McDonald's. I went back to my room and watched television till about eleven o'clock. Then I went to bed."

"Any way you can prove that? Did anyone see you?"

"Well, sure. Lots of people saw me at McDonald's but I don't know any of them. You're the only person in Moab that I know."

"Did you make any phone calls? Send any emails or texts?"

He shook his head. "No. Say, you don't think I killed that fellow, do you?"

"Not really. My goal was to rule you out as a suspect. But there's no way to verify your story." Rivera stood up and pulled his cell phone from his pocket. "Do you mind if I take a picture of you?"

"No, of course not." Ward stood up and smiled.

Rivera took a couple of snapshots.

"Say, Manny, after I'm settled in the cabin, why don't you come by and we'll do some more hikes up there?"

"Sounds like a good idea." Rivera said goodbye and returned to his vehicle.

"Did he have an alibi?" asked Gloria.

"Not really, but I just can't picture him as a killer. Let's head back to the office."

# 21

AS RIVERA AND GLORIA walked down the hallway to his office, Rivera glanced ahead through the open door of the sheriff's office. Campbell wasn't there. Probably on the golf course. Good. There'd be none of that phony fawning over Gloria. As they entered his office, his cell phone began buzzing.

He fished it out of his pocket. "Hello."

"Deputy Rivera, this is McGinty calling. I promised I'd let you know if the poachers came back. Well, they're out here now, about a mile east of my property line. I was working on that fence again when I spotted them."

"How long ago did you see them?"

"About an hour ago. Had to go back to the house to get to a telephone. Then I couldn't find the card with your telephone number on it until the missus reminded me I'd used it as a book mark in a novel I'm reading."

"How many of them did you see?"

"Three. Looked like the same bunch."

"Did you call Butch Jeffers and tell him too?" The last thing Rivera wanted was amateurs in the middle of what might turn out to be a shootout.

"Well, yes I did. I don't want that fella getting mad at me. He's ornery and mean. And me and the missus, like I told you, are out here alone."

"How long ago did you call Jeffers?"

"As soon as I got home. I'd say thirty minutes ago. I'd have called you then too but, like I said, it took me a while to find your card."

Rivera thanked him and clicked off. "The bighorn poachers are back. We need to get out there right away." He called Adam Dunne.

Dunne answered on the first ring.

"Adam, the poachers are back. Where are you?"

"I'm in Grand Junction having lunch."

"I'm leaving Moab for the Big Triangle right now. I'll be coming out BLM Route 107 and I can block their vehicle from that direction. If you can come in from the Glade Park end of 107, we can pin their vehicle in. They can't drive off road because the terrain out there is too rough."

"Will do, Manny. I'd love to get my hands on those creeps. I'm on my way."

"I expect some of those militia people will be out there too. That's going to complicate things so we need to be real careful how we handle this."

"Understood."

"Okay. See you there."

Rivera looked at Gloria. There was a fair chance of gunplay before this was over. He didn't want her to get hurt, but he also didn't want to insult her by questioning her capabilities. "Do you want to come along?"

"Of course. I'm your backup, remember? Like I said, now that I've found you, I'm not going to let anything happen to you."

"Are you *sure* you want to be part of this? You're a Rio Arriba County deputy. This is *way* beyond the call of duty."

Gloria started out of the office. "Never mind all that. We're wasting time. Let's go." She handed him his hat.

As they headed down the hallway, Rivera stopped at the office of Dave Tibbetts, a younger deputy who had helped him on several previous cases.

"Dave, I need you to come along with us. The bighorn poachers are back in action. If we move fast, we have a chance to trap them before they can escape."

Tibbetts jumped out of his chair and grabbed his hat. "I was supposed to help Sheriff Campbell at some campaign function but this is more important. And anyway, I wasn't real comfortable doing the campaign thing."

Rivera briefed him as they left the building and headed for their vehicles. "Just follow me out there. Adam Dunne is coming in from the other direction. When we see the poachers' truck—it's a gray pickup with Colorado plates—we'll stop, coordinate with Adam, and then move in on them."

They hopped into their vehicles and headed north out of Moab, turned right on Hwy 128 and drove to Roberts Bottom. They crossed the Dolores River and continued on the dirt roads, winding their way up the switchbacks to the mesa top, and continuing north. Passing the entrance to the McGinty Ranch, they turned east. A quarter mile past the Center for Cosmic Consciousness, Rivera spotted a black, extended cab pickup truck parked in a copse of juniper bushes. He recognized the vehicle—it belonged to Butch Jeffers. His worst fear had come true—the militia was about to confront the poachers. He continued a short distance and stopped when he spotted a gray pickup about a hundred yards ahead, parked alongside the road.

"We'll park here and block the poachers' exit in this direction. Adam's going to do the same thing on the other side." Rivera pulled over to the right a few feet, then motioned for Tibbetts to pull up alongside him. "Wear your body armor," he said to Tibbetts who waved in acknowledgement. Rivera turned to Gloria. "I've got an extra one for you to wear."

Rivera used his cell phone to contact Adam Dunne and learned that Dunne had just rolled to a stop a couple of hundred feet the other side of the gray pickup. "Adam, are you able to block their exit in that direction?"

"Looks like it. The road's real narrow here. Rock outcroppings on both sides. I'll park my vehicle crossways on the road. That should do it."

"Okay. Wear your body armor and let's converge at the gray pickup and plan our tactics."

Rivera, Gloria, and Tibbetts walked to the gray pickup, guns drawn and eyes scanning the rocks to their left. Adam Dunne was already there, looking in the passenger side window.

"I suppose we could just wait for them here," said Dunne. "They've got to come back to their truck sometime."

"Makes sense," said Rivera, "except those militia people are back there too. They're bound to do something stupid."

Just then, there was the sound of a rifle shot coming from the rocks, perhaps a quarter mile away. It was followed a few seconds later by two shots from a rifle that had a different sound. That was followed by unintelligible shouting and two more shots from the second gun.

"Okay," said Rivera. "It's started. Adam, you and Gloria wait here. Hide in those rocks, one on each side of their truck. If they come out, you'll be able to get the drop on them when they're out in the open between the rocks and the truck. Dave and I will circle around behind them to cut off any possible retreat." Gloria nodded in agreement, although she didn't look too happy about being left behind. But she was out of uniform and Rivera didn't want the poachers to mistake her for one of the militia members or vice versa.

"Okay," said Dunne. Let's all silence our radios and put our cell phones on vibrate so we don't give away our positions. Use cell phone communication only."

"Right," said Rivera. "McGinty said he saw three poachers and I'm guessing there are three militia types in there too. Could be more of each so be careful."

Dunne and Gloria took positions behind large rocks about twenty-five feet on either side of the truck.

Rivera and Tibbetts entered the rock field, following a barely visible animal trail. Rivera led the way with Tibbetts following. They had penetrated the rocks several hundred feet when Rivera motioned for Tibbetts to stop. They listened, hearing only the rustling of dead grama grass bending in the breeze. Rivera removed his hat, climbed partway up a large rock, and peered over the top to get a better view. He saw nothing but more rocks between him and a red rock bluff about a half mile away. Now he had to decide whether to proceed further or wait until he heard or saw something.

He decided to wait. He had a decent view across the rock field, but he realized that a lot could be taking place between the rocks. Some of the rocks were twelve to fifteen feet high, easily hiding a human. This was probably as good a viewpoint as he was going to get.

He heard voices in the distance. As the seconds ticked by, they seemed to be getting louder, closer. He couldn't make out what they were saying but the tone of voice was normal. No shouting.

Soon he could make out the words.

"Who were those guys?" said one voice.

"I dunno. Maybe hunters," said a second voice.

"Well, let them get their own bighorns," said the first.

That was followed by laughter.

"I don't think they'll be bothering us anymore," said the second voice. "After I fired at them, I'm pretty sure I heard one of them whining."

Rivera clung to the rock which concealed him, scanning the rocks and listening for any sound that might reveal the poachers' position. Then he spotted a faded blue baseball cap bobbing up and down between a couple of the rocks. A second later, it disappeared from view. The poachers were getting closer. Soon Rivera spotted them again as they passed across an opening in the rock field. They were about two hundred feet away, heading in a direction that would bring them to within fifty feet of Rivera's position as they passed by. The first man he saw was carrying a rifle. He was followed by two others who appeared to be struggling with something heavy. Then he saw a curved horn and knew they had shot and decapitated another bighorn. The sight of the animal triggered feelings of both anger and a sadness in him, but he suppressed the emotions—they would only break his concentration and interfere with his judgment.

He called Dunne and Gloria and whispered into his cell phone, warning them to be ready and telling them that three poachers were approaching, one carrying a rifle. He said he and Tibbetts would circle around behind them and follow them to the truck, cutting off any attempt at a retreat.

By the time Rivera and Tibbetts emerged from the rocks, the three poachers were standing there, hands in the air, with looks of surprise on their faces. Dunne and Gloria were holding handguns on the trio. Two of the men were in their early twenties and the third one, a bearded man, looked to be about thirty-five. A rifle was laying on the ground next to a bighorn ram's head with its amber eyes still open.

Rivera was relieved. The ambush had worked perfectly and not a single shot had been fired. And Gloria had performed her duties like the pro she was. She was standing there, knees flexed, aiming her weapon at the perps with a two-handed grip. Her badge wallet was hanging over her belt. He was proud of her.

Rivera and Tibbetts cuffed the poachers, then patted them down, removing revolvers from two of them and a black military combat knife from the third. The blade of the knife was covered with blood.

"I'd better go back in there and check on those militia people," said Rivera. "Make sure they're okay."

The bearded poacher looked at Rivera with a surprised expression and laughed out loud. "Those guys were militia?" He shook his head. "They'd better go back to militia school. I could hear one of them crying like a baby after the shooting was over."

"You shot at them?" asked Rivera.

"Damn right I shot at them. The big one fired a shot at me. Missed by a mile, but I wasn't about to let him take another shot. I fired back. I'm not sure if I hit him, but he quit firing, so maybe I got him "

"Then you'll answer for that too."

"Like hell I will. It was self-defense."

Rivera urgently needed to check on the militia members. He hoped that Butch hadn't gotten one of his young cohorts killed. Since they were trigger happy, he knew he had to be careful approaching them. He decided he'd better make his presence known. He went to his vehicle and turned on the siren for ten seconds before proceeding into the rocks.

He advanced to the same position he'd reached with Dave Tibbetts, climbed the rock, and scanned the area for a full minute. He saw no sign of human activity but thought he heard a faint squealing sound carried toward him on the breeze. He called out the names of the Jeffers brothers and James Kirtland, and listened for

a response. There was no reply. He identified himself
and shouted that the poachers were in custody and it
was safe to come out. Still no reply.

He moved ahead another forty yards through the
rocks, stopped, and listened. The squealing sound he
thought he'd heard earlier was closer now and sounded
more like high-pitched sobbing. He shouted again,
identifying himself and reiterating that the poachers
were in custody. Then he saw Kirtland peek out from
a rock about thirty yards away.

Kirtland waved his arm. "Over here, Manny. Hurry."
He sounded frightened.

Rivera picked his way through the boulder field
toward Kirtland. "James, is everyone okay?"

"No. Butch Jeffers has been shot."

Rivera saw Butch lying on his back in a sandy depression between the rocks. His brother Billy was kneeling
by his side, tears running down his cheeks. Butch was
holding his neck and Rivera could see blood on Butch's
shirt collar and his fingers.

Butch looked up at Rivera. "Help me, I've been
shot." He began sobbing. "I don't want to die."

Rivera disarmed the trio and turned his attention
to Butch. He was bleeding from a neck wound. Now
Rivera wished he'd brought along a first aid kit. He
pushed Butch's hands aside and inspected the wound.
It didn't appear to be a gunshot wound. It was a narrow,
bloody gash about a half inch long. Rivera wiped away

the blood with the tip of his index finger. Butch began squealing and wriggling as soon as Rivera touched the wound.

"Be still, Jeffers."

Rivera rubbed his bloody fingertip against his thumb and felt an abrasive substance. Sandstone. He figured one of the poacher's bullets had struck the sandstone close to where Butch was standing and sprayed tiny rock shards into his neck. Rivera wiped the wound again with his finger and a few more sandstone particles came out, but there was no sign of a bullet wound. The gash was superficial. Butch began whimpering again.

"Be quiet, Jeffers. You're not dying."

# 22

RIVERA FOLLOWED BEHIND the three militia members as they hiked along a narrow animal trail back to the road where the vehicles were parked. He thought about how foolish they had been and wondered why they didn't have enough sense to heed his warnings. He was thankful that no serious damage had been done. James Kirtland was in the lead carrying their rifles which Rivera had unloaded. Billy Jeffers was helping to guide Butch who was limping along behind Kirtland, holding a handkerchief to his neck.

The poachers were in handcuffs, sitting on the ground. The bearded poacher laughed at Butch Jeffers as he walked by.

"Militia. What a joke," he said. "They look like a bunch of losers."

The three militia members walked past him in silence, eyes fixed on the ground.

Dave Tibbetts administered first aid to Butch who seemed no longer convinced he was going to dic.

Rivera walked over to the three militia members. "You boys head back to Moab in your truck now. James, you'd better drive. Take Butch to the emergency room so they can make sure that wound doesn't get infected."

"Will do, Manny."

Just before the trio left, Rivera walked up to Butch and patted him on top of the head. He raised his voice so Butch's cohorts would be sure to hear him. "Be a good boy now, Butch. No more playing with guns." Behind Butch, Rivera saw James and Billy smile and shake their heads. That was exactly the effect Rivera was hoping for. Butch would never again be accepted as the leader of these two young men. And, hopefully, they would abandon *The Keepers of Order* and begin leading normal lives.

Butch said nothing. Subdued, he turned and headed for his vehicle. In another minute, the truck was headed back to Moab, leaving a plume of dust in its wake.

Soon thereafter, Sheila Nelson drove up in her truck. She stopped and rolled down her window. Rivera walked over to her.

"Can I get through?" she asked. Her pickup was filled with her belongings.

"I'm sorry, Sheila. It'll be another thirty or forty minutes before the road is clear. We've got to finish up here first. We just arrested the bighorn sheep poachers."

"Oh. Well, okay, I guess I'll have to wait. I just said goodbye to Brother Timothy and moved out of the cabin. I'm headed to Grand Junction and from there I'll take the Interstate to Kansas. I'm going to live with my mother for a while."

Rivera wasn't sure what to say. The girl's life had been turned upside down. "I'm real sorry about Dr. Kennedy," he managed.

"Thank you. And thanks for finding him for me." She swallowed. "That student of his, Harry Ward, started moving into the cabin as soon as I moved out. He said he was going to continue Peter's work. I know that would have pleased Peter."

"I need to get back to work. The sooner I finish, the sooner you'll be able to pass through here."

Rivera walked back to the other vehicles. Adam Dunne was struggling as he tried to lift the ram's head into the bed of his pickup.

"Adam, let me give you a hand with that." Each man grabbed a horn and hoisted the head into the pickup. Dunne began tying it down with rope.

"I guess this ram's head will end up in a museum somewhere," he said. "Or maybe at a visitor's center at one of the national parks. Look at those horns. And those eyes. What a magnificent specimen. What a shame he had to end up like this."

Rivera returned to the poachers and emptied their pockets. He opened their wallets and studied their driver's licenses. Two were from Delta, Colorado and the third was from Blanding, Utah. The leader of the group, whose name was Randolph Barnes, had a cell phone in his pocket. Rivera hoped the phone numbers it contained would reveal the identity of the bighorn buyers. He bagged and tagged the items for later study.

# 23

AS RIVERA LOADED the bags of evidence into his vehicle, he noticed that Sheila had gotten out of her pickup. He figured she was getting impatient waiting for the road to clear, but there was nothing he could do about it. She was standing there, leaning on her cane, staring at the vehicles and people blocking her passage.

He looked at Gloria. "Sheila is headed home to Kansas to live with her mother. Would you tell her we'll be done in about ten minutes?"

"Sure. There's nothing more I can do here. I'll go keep her company." Gloria walked over to Sheila and began chatting with her.

Sometime later, two additional Grand County deputies arrived and loaded the poachers into a prisoner transport vehicle. One of the deputies drove back to Moab with the prisoners and the other followed behind driving the prisoners' pickup truck.

Rivera walked over to Sheila. "We're about done here. You'll be able to leave in a minute." He noticed Gloria, who had moved behind Sheila, was shaking her head. She opened her eyes wide and looked at the ground in an exaggerated way. Rivera understood. He followed her gaze to the ground. There he saw the circular impressions the rubber tip of Sheila's cane had left in the dirt road. It was the same bull's-eye pattern Gloria had found outside Bob Livingston's trailer.

"Sheila, did you know Bob Livingston?" asked Rivera.

"Sure. He spent a month or so at the Center for Cosmic Consciousness. I got to know him a little bit during breakfast time." She smiled. "He wanted to become a famous photographer."

"Did you know him when you were both students at the University of New Mexico?"

"Well, sure, I knew who he was but I didn't know him well."

"Did you ever visit him at his home in Moab?"

Her smile faded. She shook her head. "No. Why?"

"We found impressions from your cane outside his house. We think you visited him the day he was killed."

"I did not. And plenty of people use canes."

"The rubber tip of your cane has the same bull's-eye pattern we found at Livingston's home. And the tip has that little gash in it. That's as good as a fingerprint." Rivera wasn't sure it was as good as a fingerprint but he wanted to keep the pressure on Sheila.

She opened the door of her pickup. "This is crazy. You've got no right talking to me like that." She acted like she was getting into the vehicle but instead pulled out a revolver.

"Gun!" shouted Gloria as she grabbed Sheila's wrist and threw the tiny woman face down on the ground. She twisted the gun out of Sheila's hand and held her down with a knee in her back. "Anyone got cuffs?"

Rivera smiled, impressed with Gloria's agility and technique. "I'm fresh out," he said.

Tibbetts and Dunne came running over. Tibbetts handed Gloria a set of cuffs who snapped them on Sheila's wrists. Gloria pulled Sheila to her feet, told her she was under arrest, and informed her of her rights.

"Sheila," said Rivera, "you've got a lot of explaining to do. Were you at Livingston's trailer the night he was murdered?"

She looked away from Rivera with a detached expression and gazed off into the distance. "I have nothing to say."

"You know, if the bullet that killed Livingston came from your pistol, it'll be easy enough to prove you shot him."

Her eyebrows went up a quarter inch but she remained silent.

"Let's have a look inside your vehicle," said Rivera. Underneath a tarp behind the seat was a red backpack. He pulled it out and zipped it open. Inside was an old pair of saddlebags, their leather faded and cracked. He lifted the saddlebags out, set them on the ground, and unbuckled the leather straps on one of the flaps. He pulled the compartment open and stared inside. When he saw the contents, he dumped them on the ground. There was nothing there but rocks and washers. He looked at Sheila. She was aghast.

He opened the other side of the saddlebags and dumped the contents on the ground. Again, nothing but rocks and washers.

Sheila shrieked. Her eyes moved wildly in her head. "My God, I killed him for nothing. For nothing!"

# 24

DAVE TIBBETTS LEFT for Moab with a stunned Sheila Nelson in handcuffs, and Adam Dunne said goodbye and headed for the BLM office with the ram's head. Rivera and Gloria were left there alone, now removing their body armor.

"I believe we're finished here," said Rivera. He smiled and looked at Gloria. He was impressed with her. "Thanks for a job well done. You broke the Livingston case wide open."

She grinned. "Glad to help."

"Nothing left to do here. Might as well head back to town."

"Good. I'm hungry and you promised me dinner."

They hopped into Rivera's vehicle and headed west. As they neared the entrance to the McGinty Ranch, Rivera decided to make a quick detour. He turned into the ranch and drove down the dirt road to the ranch house. The McGintys were sitting on the porch. Rivera got out of the vehicle and walked over to them. Mrs. McGinty watched him with a worried frown.

"We heard some shooting in the distance a while ago," said Mr. McGinty, standing up. "We were kind of concerned."

"Yeah. That's what I stopped by to tell you about. We've caught the poachers and arrested them, so you won't have to worry about them anymore. And I doubt Butch Jeffers will ever bother you again. I think his militia members have probably abandoned him."

"I'm so relieved," said Mrs. McGinty. "Those militia people had me scared to death. We ain't had no peace since the day they showed up here."

Mr. McGinty shook Rivera's hand. "Thank you."

On the drive back to Moab, Rivera and Gloria were silent, alone in their thoughts. As they crossed the Dolores River, Rivera broke the silence.

"I was just thinking about Sheila's behavior whenever I spoke with her. She always seemed so concerned about Dr. Kennedy. She sure had me fooled."

"Don't forget," said Gloria, she was an actress in the Drama Club in college. Remember the Desdemona photograph in Livingston's yearbook?"

"Oh yeah, I'd forgotten about that. I'll have to give her high marks for acting."

"Well, both your cases are solved now. Maybe you can relax a little."

"I'll have to process the prisoners first. Then finish up my reports. After that, we can have a nice dinner somewhere."

"I'll tell you what. While you're finishing up your paperwork, I'll go to City Market and pick up some groceries. Tonight, you get a home cooked meal."

Rivera grinned. "Really? Sounds good to me."

They fell silent again for several minutes. "Something's bothering you, Manny. What is it?"

"The rocks and washers we found in the saddlebags. They came from Livingston's rock collection and those bags of hardware he used in creating sculptures."

"Right. So?"

"What happened to the gold coins?"

"Good question. Do you think maybe Livingston hid them somewhere and refilled the saddlebags with the rocks and washers?"

"I don't know. Maybe I'll learn more after I question Sheila. Since she's admitted to killing Livingston, she's got no reason to withhold any of the details."

"I hope you're right. I'd like to know exactly what happened."

# 25

RIVERA DROVE HOME and dropped Gloria off, then returned to the office. Adam Dunne was waiting there for him.

"Hi, Manny. Good job out there today."

"You too, Adam. Thanks for the help."

"John Singleton said to thank you. Now his bighorn program in the Big Triangle can get back on track."

"I've been checking on the poachers. It appears Randolph Barnes, their leader, has been arrested before. The other two seem to be just hired hands. Barnes claims they were out there hiking and *found* the ram's head. Can you believe that? *Found* it. He said someone took a shot at him and he fired back in self-defense. He also said he's got a good lawyer, so he isn't worried. We might have a hard time proving anything here."

"We may have to hunt for the ram's carcass and extract the bullet that killed it. See if it's a match for Barnes's rifle. If it is, we'll have a good case. Also, the blood on that knife his accomplice was carrying is probably a match for the ram's blood."

"Yeah. All that's probably going to be necessary. Meanwhile, they'll be out on bail. Probably killing bighorn rams somewhere else. It's discouraging. What did you do with the ram's head?"

"I dropped it off at the BLM office. A taxidermist is on his way to preserve it. He's going to save a sample of the animal's blood in case a comparison with the blood on the knife is needed."

After Dunne left, Rivera went to the holding cell area. The three poachers were in one cell, Sheila in another. Sheila looked even smaller than usual as she sat huddled on the bench in the corner of the cell, clutching her knees to her chest and staring at the floor. Rivera brought her to an interrogation room which had one straight back chair on each side of a metal table.

They sat down, Sheila slouching in her chair with her arms folded across her chest. She was frowning and her eyes were fixed on Rivera.

"I'd like to ask you a few questions," Rivera began.

"Why you?" she asked.

"What do you mean?"

"Why are you questioning me? Why not the lady cop?"

"Would you rather be questioned by a lady cop?"

"I've been mistreated by men my whole life. First my father, then my boyfriend, then Peter Kennedy, then Bob Livingston, and now you. I don't trust men anymore."

Rivera softened his voice. "I'm not going to mistreat you, Sheila. I just want to ask you some questions. We know you killed Bob Livingston but now I'm trying to piece together what happened—what the sequence of events was. That's all. There are a lot of things I don't understand. I thought maybe you could help me."

Her facial expression relaxed and her voice softened. "You want my help?"

Rivera was startled by the question. It was like a toggle switch had been thrown inside Sheila's brain. Gone was the attitude. Suddenly she seemed pleasant and willing to help. It was as though one part of her brain mistrusted men and the other part was eager to please them. It occurred to him that she might be in need of psychiatric help. He decided to probe slowly, gently. "What happened between you and your father?"

"I was very close to my father. I loved being with him. Every day after school when I was a little girl, I'd wait for him to come home from work so I could sit on his lap, talk with him, and tell him about my day. I followed him around the house like a puppy. I did everything I could to please him—bring him the newspaper, get his slippers, even bring him a beer. He loved his beer—probably drank too much of it but I didn't care. I just wanted to spend time with him. He was my whole world. Then one day, I came home from school and found my mother crying. She was holding a note in her hand. She told me that Daddy had left us and gone away. We never saw him again. To this day, I don't know what I did to make him leave me."

Rivera shook his head. That had to be a traumatic event in young Sheila's life. "That's very sad. What happened with your boyfriend?"

"His name was Paul. He was my crush in sophomore year at the university. I thought he was going to be the man in my life forever. He led me to believe that one day we would be married. He was the first man I was intimate with. Then one day, he announced that it was over. He'd found someone else he liked better. It was like getting kicked in the stomach. I still think about him."

"What about Dr. Kennedy?"

She thought for a moment. "Well, when Peter left the cabin that day ..."

Rivera smiled and raised his hand. "If you don't mind, Sheila, could you start at the beginning? Back when you were a student at the university?"

Sheila grinned and bounced lightly in her chair. "Sure. I was a student working on my degree in anthropology. I was in two of Peter's classes. He was real popular because he made everything so interesting. He was kind of a showman in the classroom. Very animated, very dramatic. I knew he was interested in me because I caught him looking at me a few times, but he was too old for me. Besides I had started seeing Bob Livingston at the time."

"You dated Livingston back in school?"

"Yes. After Paul. Bob was kind of a loner. Always had a forlorn expression on his face like he was struggling with some kind of internal problem—a look of quiet anguish like an artist might have. I think that's what attracted me to him. He always had a camera hanging around his neck. He said his life's goal was to become a famous photographer. He was studying anthropology because he loved Native American dwellings, petroglyphs, ceramic pots, and artifacts. He wanted the theme of his photographic work to be America before the white man arrived. I fell for him and we dated for a few months. I had no idea then how dishonest he was."

"So then you started dating Dr. Kennedy?"

"Not right away. He would see me in the cafeteria and sit down across from me and talk. He paid a lot of attention to me. He told me his wife had passed away three years earlier and sometimes he got lonely. He just wanted someone to talk to. One day, he asked me if I'd like to come to his apartment and see his collection of early-American pottery. I was curious, so I accepted his invitation. The collection was impressive but I had the feeling he just wanted someone to listen to his problems. He offered me a drink which I sipped on slowly. He drank a couple and then poured himself a third one. As he loosened up, he started talking about his career and the problems he was having professionally. I was surprised because I never dreamed someone of his stature would have professional problems. The problem centered on the petroglyph theories he had put forward. Most of his peers had rejected his theories and Peter's status had changed from rising star to intellectual pariah. His hoped-for appointment as a tenured professor was in serious jeopardy. Then he told me he had decided to leave the university at the end of the semester."

"How did you feel when he told you about that?"

"I felt sorry for him. He told me to keep everything secret and that I was the only one he had confided in. That made me feel close to him. We started seeing each other secretly after that but somehow the word got out and that made his problems even worse."

"What happened with Bob Livingston?"

"We just stopped seeing each other. He seemed like a child compared to Peter. I think Bob was hurt and angry, but he never said anything about it. He just went away quietly."

"So you kept seeing Dr. Kennedy."

"Yes. We saw each other a lot. For me, it was just a companionship thing, but I knew he wanted it to be more than that. Then, one day, he told me about the gold coins he'd found during one of his field trips. He said he'd found a series of shaman petroglyphs, all made by the same Ute medicine man, which led to a saddlebag full of Spanish gold coins. He said they were worth millions. Peter liked to refer to the treasure as the 'shaman's secret.' My folks were poor so I'd never known a millionaire before. He said he wanted me to come with him when he left the university and that he wanted to take care of me. He'd learned about the Center for Cosmic Consciousness and the availability of an off-the-grid cabin on the property. I liked the idea of never having to worry about money again. We became lovers and when he left the university, I went with him." She emitted a high-pitched giggle. "To be honest, I couldn't wait to get my hands on that gold."

"If you had gotten your hands on the gold, what would you have done?"

She thought. "I'd probably have been out of there in a New York minute."

"So you moved to the cabin."

"Right. It was fun for a few days but it became boring pretty quick. He was into his research and didn't pay a whole lot of attention to me. I tried to get interested in his work but couldn't. I wanted to go exploring with him, looking for new petroglyphs, but my knee made hiking on that rugged terrain impossible. I wanted to leave but I didn't want to go away empty handed. I felt I had a right to some of that gold. He owed me that. When I asked him if I could have some of it, he said no. He said he was slowly selling the coins and donating the proceeds to charity. He said money ruined people and he planned to give it all away to organizations that help poor but promising kids make it through college.

I wasn't sure if he was really doing that or simply selling the coins and depositing the money in his bank account."

"He refused to give you any of it?'

"Worse than that. He began taunting me about it when we were alone in the cabin. He knew I had no place else to go. I was broke and all I had was a Bachelor's degree in anthropology. Who would hire me with only that? He knew I depended on him for support, so he used the money to keep me there with him. He would give me subtle reminders every day that he was my sole means of support and that I was lucky to have someone of his stature providing for me. Our relationship was going downhill fast. I grew to hate him but I had to hide my feelings. I wanted to follow him to the gold but couldn't. I decided to take matters into my own hands and get that gold. I knew Bob Livingston was living in Moab, so one day when I went grocery shopping there, I looked him up. I told him I knew where there was a stash of gold coins but couldn't get to them myself because of my knee. He was immediately interested. We formed a 50-50 partnership."

"Is that why Livingston moved to the Center?"

"Yes. The plan was for Bob to follow Peter each day he went out into the backcountry. Bob was strong and agile, so I knew he'd have no trouble keeping up with Peter. I never knew on what particular day Peter would go to the saddlebags and retrieve a coin to sell, so Bob had to follow him each day. Finally, Bob located the hiding place. The one thing I never expected was that Bob would kill Peter. That's certainly not something I intended. Bob should have been more patient—locate the gold, wait till Peter left, and then take the gold. But no, he had to go and kill Peter." Sheila's eyes welled up with tears. Then she chuckled. "I guess I had some feelings for Peter after all."

"Then, three days after Peter was killed, you went to visit Bob?"

"Yes. I went to his trailer to get my half of the treasure. I took Peter's handgun with me just in case Bob decided not to give me an even split. I thought he might say he did all the work and deserved more than half. I wasn't planning on having to shoot him, but I thought I might have to scare him into keeping his end of the bargain. When I got there, Bob had just returned from the gallery that was exhibiting his photographs. He was happy and pumped up about his career as a photographer. When I asked him about the gold coins, he said I had no right to any of it. He'd done all the work and he'd committed murder for it. And he said I'd better keep my mouth shut about the whole business because I was an accessory to murder. He started taunting me just the way Peter did. Said something about me being a gold digger and that I'd always be poor and dependent. Then he reminded me that I'd left him back in college to be with Dr. Kennedy. He kept digging at me until I lost my temper. He laughed and pointed to a red backpack on the floor and said the saddlebags were in there and they were full of gold coins, but I'd never get to see any of them. I pulled out the pistol and pointed it at him. He kept laughing and said I didn't have the courage to do anything for myself, much less shoot a man. He took a step toward me and reached for the gun. I shot him dead." Sheila quivered for a moment, then emitted a shrill, almost maniacal laugh. "I'd finally had enough of men taking advantage of me."

Rivera thought about the gold coins. "What do you think happened to the gold coins?"

"I don't know. I assumed the saddlebags were full of them. I was planning to look at them after I got to Kansas. I was stupid not to have checked sooner. I freaked out when you emptied the saddlebags on the ground and I saw what was actually in them. Now my life is ruined. And for what? A bunch of rocks and washers." Her face froze with an expression of horror, as though she had just comprehended the full extent of her actions. She stared blankly past Rivera and fell silent, never uttering another word.

# 26

AFTER RETURNING SHEILA to her jail cell, Rivera detoured by the break room and picked up a mug of coffee. He closed the door to his office and updated his reports on the bighorn poaching and the murders of Dr. Kennedy and Bob Livingston. Then he leaned back, hoisted his feet onto his desk, and stared out the window at the snow-capped peaks of the LaSal Mountains. He should have been satisfied—both of his cases had been solved—but instead he had an unsettled feeling. The problem was that each case had a major loose end. The gold from the saddlebags hadn't been accounted for and the people at the buying end of the bighorn poaching operation hadn't yet been identified. Rivera disliked loose ends. They kept him awake at night.

He decided to focus on the poaching problem first. The pickup truck used by the poachers had been searched. Nothing useful had been turned up. It was registered in the name of Randolph Barnes, the bearded leader of the trio. Rivera thought about what Barnes had said—that they had found the ram's head and that he had fired at the militia members in self-defense. Rivera worried that the arrest of the trio might not stick. He needed more.

On his desk were the evidence bags containing the contents of the poachers' pockets. He searched through their wallets and found nothing incriminating. Then he picked up the cell phone that belonged to Barnes and turned it on. It asked for a passcode. Rivera wondered if Barnes did what Rivera himself did—select a passcode that was easy to key in. Rivera used the digits 2-5-8-0 to unlock his cell phone. The four digits were straight down the center of the numeric keypad thereby making it easy to enter the code while driving. Gloria and a few of his fellow deputies used the same code. He punched in 2-5-8-0 and he smiled as an array of icons appeared on the screen. He studied the icons for a few minutes, seeing nothing unusual. Then he checked the list of recent calls. One number which appeared frequently on the list jumped out at him. It had the Moab area code and prefix. The calls were both incoming and outgoing. A quick check of the cross directory yielded a name that shocked Rivera. The number belonged to Charlie Baxter, John Singleton's technical assistant who had designed the bighorn sheep tracking system. Rivera sat back and shook his head. No wonder the poachers had no problem finding the herds. Baxter had day to day location information transmitted from the rams' collars via satellite to his computer.

Rivera picked up the phone and punched in Adam Dunne's cell phone number.

"Adam, are you in your office?'

"Yeah. I'm updating my report on the poaching operation." He sounded tired.

"Are you sitting down?"

"Of course. I don't normally do my typing standing up."

"I think I know why the poachers have been so successful at locating the bighorn herds."

"Really? Tell me."

Rivera explained what he had learned from the call log on the poacher's cell phone. "It seems the BLM has a mole in its operation. Charlie Baxter has been in regular contact with Randolph Barnes."

"Why that little sonofabitch. I'm gonna go over there and kill him."

"Hold on, big fella. Let's just arrest him. And if you can hold your horses for a few minutes, I'd like to be there when you cuff him. I want to see the look on his face."

"Okay, Manny, but you'd better hurry. I'm not sure how long I can hold off."

Rivera left his office and drove to the BLM Field Office building. Dunne was waiting for him at the front door. "Okay, Adam, do you want to do the honors?"

"Gladly. But let's get John Singleton in on it first so he's not blindsided. Baxter is his only employee and I know John thinks highly of him. He couldn't function without him."

Rivera and Dunne went to Singleton's office and closed the door. Singleton's jaw dropped when Dunne gave him the news.

"I just can't believe it," said Singleton, shaking his head. "He's been working with me for three years. I had no idea. Are you sure?"

"There's no question that he's been in touch with the poachers," said Rivera.

"I'm going to arrest him now," said Dunne. "Do you want to come with us, John?"

Singleton's expression was grim and he thought for a long moment. He slowly pushed himself out of his chair. "Not really, but I guess I should be there."

The three men walked down the hall and entered Baxter's small laboratory. Baxter was sitting at his desk, talking on his cell phone. He finished what sounded like a personal conversation, dropped the phone into his shirt pocket, and smiled.

"Gentlemen, welcome to the magic world of electronics. How may I help you?"

"Mind if I look at your cell phone, Charlie?" asked Dunne.

"Uh, well, why?"

"I want to see who you've been calling lately." Dunne had a fierce look on his face. Rivera was worried Dunne was going to lose it and stepped closer to him, just in case restraint was necessary.

"Adam, I don't believe you have the right to look at my personal phone calls," said Baxter.

"We captured the poachers. Their cell phone showed a long series of calls between you and them. It's been going on for months."

Baxter looked stunned. His face turned red. He looked at Singleton and then back at Dunne. "There must be some mistake."

"No mistake. You're under arrest, you little bastard." Dunne Mirandized him. Then he cuffed him and not in a gentle way. He emptied Baxter's pockets and bagged everything except his cell phone. Since Baxter had just been talking on his cell phone, it was still unlocked, so no passcode was necessary. A quick check of his phone log revealed that he had, in fact, called Randolph Barnes many times in recent months. There was no mistake.

Rivera and Dunne returned to the sheriff's office and placed Baxter, whose face remained red throughout, into an empty cell. "This place is filling up," said Dunne.

"Let's go to my office," said Rivera. "There are a number of out of state calls on Barnes's cell phone. I'm guessing some of those numbers belong to the hunting ranches which have been buying the bighorn rams from Barnes. Let's send that info to your friend in the FBI and let the feds handle it. Maybe they can make some quick arrests at those ranches."

"Good idea. I think they'll be a lot more interested now that we've rounded up the poachers."

As he was driving home, Rivera was confident the bighorn operation had been put to a stop, at least on the poaching end. Now he could close the books on that case. On the other case, he knew that Bob Livingston had wounded Zeke Stanton and killed Dr. Peter Kennedy, and that Sheila Nelson had killed Bob Livingston. But the remainder of the gold coins was still unaccounted for. He was tired and knew Gloria was waiting for him with a home cooked meal. He decided he'd worry about the gold tomorrow.

When Rivera walked through the front door of his house, the first thing that struck him was the smell of something delicious cooking in the kitchen. Then Bentley, his chocolate Labrador retriever, came bounding up to him, wagging his tail with enthusiasm, and licking Rivera's hand. Rivera knelt down and gave the dog a hug and received an ear licking in return.

"Bentley missed you," said Gloria from the kitchen. "So did I," she added as she came to Rivera and gave him a hug.

"Avoid the left ear area," said Rivera. "Bentley's already been there."

She laughed and gave him a lingering, passionate kiss on the lips.

"What a nice welcome home. I could get used to this," he said. And he meant it.

Gloria's mouth opened as if to respond, but instead she just smiled, gave Rivera another hug, and returned to the kitchen.

Rivera took a quick shower and changed his clothes while Gloria finished preparing their meal. During dinner, Rivera told her about the arrest of Charlie Baxter and the long-distance telephone numbers found in Barnes's cell phone.

"Adam Dunne forwarded those phone numbers to his friend in the FBI. Hopefully, the feds will get right on the case and make some arrests before word gets out that we've captured the poachers."

"You mean before the ranch operators learn about the arrests and cover their tracks."

"Exactly. I'm sure those ranches must keep accounting records of the ram purchases, which hunters shot them, and what they paid for the privilege. Those records would disappear in a heartbeat if the ranch operators knew the poachers were in custody."

Soft music filled the room while they enjoyed a meal of pork roast topped with mushrooms in gravy, brown rice, and green beans. Gloria had selected a Zinfandel to go with the meal. Rivera felt a contentment he wasn't used to.

"Well, my time here has gone fast," she said when the meal was over. "I'll be leaving for New Mexico in the morning. Sheriff Gallegos wants me back on the job day after tomorrow."

Rivera wiped his lips with his napkin. "I'm sure sorry I had to work the whole time you were here. We'll have to schedule those hikes for your next visit."

"Oh, Manny, nothing could have been more fun for me than helping you on your case. We got to spend a lot of time together and I had another chance to see how you work. I had a ball."

"And if it weren't for you, Sheila Nelson would be in Kansas by now. Great job spotting the imprint of her cane at Livingston's trailer and again out in the Big Triangle. I'll work with you anytime."

"We make a good team."

Later that evening, they sat on the couch in front of the television, watching the election returns coming in.

"The vote tally for Sheriff Campbell is looking pretty bleak," said Gloria. "He's losing by a wide margin."

"Yeah. I kind of feel sorry for him for a lot of reasons, but the truth is he doesn't belong in the job of sheriff. Looks like Louise Anderson will be my new boss."

Rivera yawned. It was time for bed. He loved having Gloria stay with him, and, at this moment, gold coins were the farthest thing from his mind.

# 27

RIVERA WATCHED AS Gloria's vehicle pulled away from the curb in front of his house. She blew him a kiss through the open window. He had a feeling of emptiness as he stood on his front lawn and watched her drive the two blocks to Main Street, turn left, and disappear from view.

Ten minutes later, He pulled out of his driveway and drove to the sheriff's office. His thoughts were focused on how much he would miss Gloria, how empty his house would feel without her in it, and how long the next three weeks would seem until he drove to Abiquiu to be with her again. It was the same feeling he had at the end of each of their visits.

He parked his vehicle in front of the sheriff's building and entered. As he walked down the hallway to his office, he spotted Sheriff Denny Campbell. He was boxing up some things in his office, which seemed unusual since he had seven more weeks to serve before his term was up. Rivera continued down the hall to Campbell's office. He was glad Campbell was no longer his boss, but he wanted to wish him the best. Campbell looked up from the box he was packing and frowned.

"Did you come to gloat?"

Rivera wasn't expecting a comment like that. "No. I just came by to wish you the best."

Campbell shook his head. "I can't believe that old broad beat me." He was removing framed pictures from the walls and throwing them in one of the boxes. "And you bear part of the responsibility. If you had helped me campaign, I'd probably have won the election."

Rivera didn't know what to say. He just shrugged and left Campbell's office. Campbell was muttering incoherently as Rivera walked down the hall. He detoured by the break room and picked up a mug of coffee. He closed the door to his office, sat down at his desk, and took a sip. Thankfully, the Campbell era was coming to a close.

His telephone rang. The caller was Adam Dunne.

"How does it feel to have a new boss?"

"I haven't talked to her yet."

"Bound to be an improvement. How's Campbell taking it?"

"He's already started cleaning out his office. Blames me for his loss."

"Well, that's as it should be. I blame you for all my problems. He might as well, too."

Rivera laughed. "You should treat me a little better since I'm always doing your work for you."

"Manny, guess what?"

"It's too early in the morning for guessing."

"I just got a call from my FBI friend. Most of the long-distance numbers stored in Randolph Barnes's cell phone belong to two big game hunting ranches. One in eastern New Mexico and one in west Texas. Both ranches belong to the same guy—a former Texas state senator from Fort Worth. The feds got a warrant and searched both places early this morning. They found an electronic collar that was formerly worn by one of the Big Triangle bighorn rams. They also found business records containing hunter's names, what kind of animal they shot, and how much they paid. Bighorns had been hunted and killed on both ranches. They also found taxidermy records for bighorns. It's an airtight case."

"That's great. I only hope the ranch owner gets more than a slap on the wrist. They need to make an example of him."

"I agree. We'll see."

After Rivera hung up, he sat back and took another sip of coffee. The bighorn poaching case no longer required his attention, but there was still the question of what had become of the gold coins. Rivera assumed his standard thinking position—feet on the desk, hands clasped behind his head, eyes staring through the window at the LaSal Mountains. The gold had been removed from the saddlebags and replaced with rocks and washers—presumably the rocks for the weight and the washers for the sound of jingling coins. Sylvia, the owner of the Cenizo Art Gallery, had said Livingston was at the photograph exhibition that evening, so the switch must have taken place after he went to the gallery and before Sheila Nelson killed him and made off with the saddlebags. So who could have known about the coins and their location in Livingston's trailer? Certainly, Sheila Nelson knew but all she got was rocks and washers. And it was unlikely Livingston had discussed the coins with anyone else. Why would he? It was in his best interest to keep their existence secret.

Rivera thought about that a long time. Somebody had to have figured out the whole scheme. But how could the thief have done that? Rivera couldn't think of a way, unless the thief had figured it out the same way Rivera himself did. He reviewed the sequence of events which had led him to the conclusion that Livingston had killed Dr. Kennedy and taken the gold. The key had been the photograph of the handholds in the Cenizo Art Gallery. He pictured the photograph there, hanging on the wall, and the visitors milling about in the gallery. A smile slowly came to his face. He laughed and shook his head. Could it be?

He grabbed his hat and headed for the gallery in his pickup.

Sylvia was just opening up. She smiled when she saw him. "Can I interest you in a fine photograph?"

"Not today, Sylvia, I'm here on business. Do you still have the visitor's log book from the Art Walk exhibit?"

"Sure."

"I'd like to see it."

"No problem. I'll get it for you." She left and returned with the book.

Rivera sat down in a visitor's chair and paged through it. The log for the day of Livingston's murder was sixteen pages long. Some two hundred people had visited the gallery that day. He found his own signature and worked back through the earlier entries. Ten pages back, he found what he was looking for. He smiled and nodded. Harry Ward's name was at the bottom of page three. Harry had failed to mention to Rivera that, besides dinner at McDonald's and watching TV in his motel room, he had also visited the Cenizo Gallery. Ward had solved the mystery the same way Rivera did.

Ward had visited the cliff dwelling the day after Rivera had found Kennedy's body there, so he knew what the handholds looked like. He'd probably photographed them just as Rivera had. By happenstance, Harry had participated in the Art Walk. Then, when he saw Livingston's handholds photograph at the gallery, he'd noticed the footprint pattern and reached the same conclusion Rivera had—two sets of footprints, one belonging to Kennedy and one belonging to the killer. No third set of prints belonging to Rivera. And finding out where Livingston lived was no problem.

He was listed in the local telephone book. Rivera remembered that Harry had mentioned one of his past jobs had been working for a locksmith company. That meant picking the lock to Livingston's trailer would have been child's play for him. Chris Carey had quoted his professor friend at the University of New Mexico as having said that Ward had an exceptional mind. Rivera nodded to himself. No question about it—Ward was one smart fellow.

Rivera got up and walked over to Sylvia who was dusting off an ornate frame containing a photograph of a dagger yucca backlighted by a full moon.

"Do you remember what time Bob Livingston arrived at the gallery during the Art Walk exhibit?" he asked.

"Oh, that poor boy. It's so sad what happened to him." She thought for a long moment. "I'd say he arrived about four in the afternoon. He was *so* looking forward to meeting our patrons and possibly selling some copies of his photographs."

"How long did he stay here?"

She thought again. "He left a little after seven o'clock."

Rivera extracted his cell phone and showed Sylvia the pictures he'd taken of Harry Ward at the Ramada Inn swimming pool. "Do you remember seeing this fellow that night?"

Sylvia peered at the photo. "Why yes. He had a long conversation with Bob Livingston and left the gallery shortly afterwards."

"Thanks, Sylvia. You've been a big help."

Rivera rechecked the log. Harry had arrived early and probably left soon after seeing Livingston's photograph. Since Livingston was at the exhibit, Ward knew he wouldn't be at home. After locating Livingston's trailer and picking the lock, he would have spotted the red backpack, opened it, and found the saddlebags. After transferring the coins to his own container, probably a backpack, he loaded some rocks from Livingston's rock collection and washers from his sculpture supplies into the saddlebags. The whole process wouldn't have taken more than a couple of minutes. But why did Harry bother to load the rocks and washers into the saddlebags? Was it for fun? Intrigue? Maybe he didn't want Livingston to realize the coins had been taken until Harry had time to leave town. That part puzzled Rivera. Would Livingston have suspected Harry? And if so, why?

Rivera called Brother Timothy at the Center for Cosmic Consciousness and asked if Ward had checked into the off-the-grid cabin. Brother Timothy said yes and added that Ward was at the cabin now.

# 28

RIVERA DROVE TO the Center for Cosmic Consciousness, wondering how Harry Ward would react to his unannounced visit—or how he would respond to Rivera's questioning about the gold coins. Would he open up when Rivera questioned him or would he simply deny the allegations? And if he did deny them, what would Rivera do then? He had no answer for that. Rivera wasn't even sure how he would begin the questioning. Maybe just ask Ward outright. Never knowing what had actually happened to the gold would bother Rivera for the rest of his life, so he was determined to learn the truth.

He continued on the two-track to the off-the-grid cabin. Harry Ward, wearing jeans and a rust-colored T-shirt, was outside feeding the chickens. Ward looked up and grinned as Rivera pulled up and got out of his vehicle.

"Welcome to my new home." Ward made an all-encompassing gesture that included the cabin, chicken coop, outhouse, solar array, and windmill. "And I guess I've inherited these fine chickens."

"Yeah, I can see that." Rivera got right to the point. "Harry, I'd like to know what you did with those gold coins."

Ward's grin disappeared. It was replaced by a pensive stare. He sat down on the cabin steps and studied Rivera's face for a long time. "You wearing a wire?"

Rivera dragged over a yard chair and sat down facing Ward. "No, Harry, I'm not wearing a wire. We don't even *have* wires at the Grand County Sheriff's Office."

"I'm trying to decide whether to tell you what I know."

"I need to know, Harry."

Ward nodded. "I imagine you do. All right, Manny, I'll tell you, but if you ever bring charges against me, of course I'll deny this conversation ever took place. Agreed?"

Rivera nodded. "Agreed."

Ward took a deep breath and let it out. "It all goes back to my association with Dr. Kennedy at the university. I thought the world of him. My father was a hardworking man. He worked in the retail lumber business. He was a loyal employee, but he was always worried about losing his job. The industry was consolidating and the big companies were driving the locals out of business, so he spent a lot of extra time at work—ten hours a day, six days a week. At home, he was always tired and worried. Didn't have much time for me. I don't think I was being selfish. It was just that the other kids' fathers were teaching them sports and helping them learn about life, and I wasn't getting any of that. So when I met Dr. Kennedy and he took an interest in me, I felt like I was getting the attention I missed as a kid. I loved my father, of course. He was a good man and a good provider, but Dr. Kennedy filled a void in me that needed filling."

"You first met him at the University of New Mexico?"

"Right. It was my senior year. I found his work fascinating and he enjoyed talking to me about it. We would meet after class a couple of times a week and he would tell me about his latest theory or recent artifact discovery, and show me photographs of his backcountry adventures. It was after I got to know him that I decided I wanted to specialize in anthropology."

Rivera was eager for Harry to get to the point about the gold, but he didn't want to break the rhythm of his story. Besides, he found Ward's relationship with Kennedy interesting. "So the friendship carried all the way to graduate school?"

"Yes. We became closer. More like family than teacher and student. Then Dr. Kennedy came under attack by some of his associates at the university and in the anthropological societies because of his theories about the Fremont and Ute cultures, and because he was seeing Sheila who was one of his students. I already told you some of that. I believed they were all jealous of him. I wanted to help defend him but I didn't know how. I was just a student—no one would have taken me seriously. I was crushed the day he told me he'd decided to leave the university. A couple of weeks later, he told me about the petroglyphs he'd found which he believed were made by a Ute medicine man. You know that story. The medicine man killed a Spaniard and took his saddlebags. He hid them in a safe place to keep the white man's bad medicine from harming the members of his tribe. Dr. Kennedy told me that if anything happened to him, he wanted me to finish what he'd started. He was bequeathing his life's work to me. I was astonished and flattered. I felt like I really *was* his son."

"What about the gold coins?" As soon as Rivera asked that question, he regretted it. This wasn't the time for impatience. Hopefully Harry would get to that part of the story in due course.

Harry smiled. "Manny, I'm giving you the whole story so you'll understand why I did what I did. I like you and I think you have a right to know. When you understand everything, I think you'll agree that I did nothing wrong."

"Okay, Harry. Sorry for the interruption. Please continue."

"He invited me to visit him at the Center for Cosmic Consciousness, so I came to Moab. That's when I met you. You and I followed the shaman petroglyphs to the cliff dwelling and that's where you found Dr. Kennedy's body." Harry's voice broke and he choked up for a moment. "You wouldn't let me enter the area because you didn't want the crime scene disturbed, so I came back the next day. I climbed the handholds up to the cliff dwelling and saw the impressions in the dirt floor that looked like they could have been made by saddlebags. So I knew that whoever killed Dr. Kennedy had taken the bags. By happenstance, I went to the art gallery and saw Bob Livingston's photo. And yes, I lied to you about being in my motel room watching television that evening. Sorry about that. When I saw the footprint patterns in the photograph, I reached the same conclusion you probably did—that whoever had taken that photograph had also killed Dr. Kennedy and made off with the saddlebags. Livingston was at the gallery, talking with some of the patrons. I struck up a conversation with him, asking what I hoped seemed like innocuous questions. I asked him where he found the handholds, but he dodged the question. He chatted me up, wanting to know if I'd be interested in buying a copy of the photo. I said I'd think about it. He gave me his card, which, of course had his address on it. Then the owner of the gallery walked up and asked Livingston how much longer he planned to be there. She had some art lovers coming that she said he should meet. He told her he'd be there at least two more hours."

Ward stopped. He looked at Rivera as if making sure the deputy was following all this. Rivera nodded for him to continue.

"So there it was. I had two hours to find his home and see if the gold coins were there. And it was easy. I found his trailer, picked the lock, and entered with a backpack I kept in my truck. I wore gloves so there would be no fingerprints. I saw Livingston's dusty red backpack on the floor and opened it. There were the saddlebags. I opened them up and couldn't believe my eyes—inside were hundreds of old Spanish coins. The glittering gold took my breath away. After I recovered from the adrenalin rush, I transferred the coins by the handful into my backpack until I had every last one of them. Before I left, I reloaded the saddlebags with some of the rocks and washers I'd found in Livingston's trailer, and then closed everything up. I made sure his backpack was still in the same place on the floor. I didn't want him to realize the coins had been taken until much later. I knew he was a killer and he might remember me from the gallery and put two and two together. Then I split."

Rivera considered that. When Livingston returned home later, there would be no reason for him to open his backpack and check the coins. His backpack was still there, in the same place he'd left it. Sheila would have arrived at Livingston's trailer a little later, asking for her share of the gold. Livingston taunted her, which, because of her past history, infuriated her.

When he reneged on their deal, she shot him, took the backpack, and left. The sound of the washers jingling inside the backpack must have reassured her that she had the coins.

"And what did you do with the coins?"

Harry grinned. "I hid them in the rocky backcountry within a couple of miles of where they had rested for over two centuries. No one will ever find them. I think that's what Dr. Kennedy would have wanted. Now I plan to stay in this cabin, live simply, and lead my life just the way he did. I'll continue his research, and when I have enough information to prove his theories, I'll publish them. Then I'll take great pleasure in watching his critics eat crow. And believe me, I'll do it to cause maximum embarrassment to each one of them. I'll do whatever I can to destroy their professional reputations."

Rivera wasn't sure what to do about the coins. "You know, Harry, those coins don't belong to you."

Harry looked at Rivera for a long moment. "Tell me this, Manny. To whom do the coins belong? Bob Livingston? Dr. Kennedy? The Ute medicine man? The Spanish Conquistador? The Native Americans from whom the Spaniards stole the gold? The U.S. Government who stole these lands from Mexico? Who do you think is the rightful owner?"

Rivera had no answer. He stood up. "To tell you the truth Harry, I have no idea."

"Are you going to arrest me for stealing the coins from Livingston?"

Rivera shook his head. "There's no way I can prove you took them."

# 29

RIVERA HAD JUST finished telling Chris Carey the whole story of how Dr. Kennedy had found the gold coins and how Bob Livingston and Sheila Nelson had conspired to take them from him. They were sitting at an outdoor table at the Jailhouse Cafe, enjoying lunch and each other's company. Rivera was eating a BLT on toast and Carey had settled for a plate of ham and eggs. It was a mild day with temperatures in the low seventies. The sun slanted through the overhead arbor producing dappled shadows on the table.

"You know what puzzles me about the whole Livingston affair?" asked Carey. "Why, after killing Dr. Kennedy and retrieving the saddlebags from the cliff dwelling, would Livingston stop and take a photograph of those handholds in the cliff wall?'

"I guess he must have had a genuine artist's temperament," said Rivera. "Becoming a world class photographer was his life's goal, and handholds leading up to an ancient cliff dwelling would be prime subject matter. Given enough time, he might have achieved his goal. Too bad Sheila had to come along and tempt him with gold."

Carey shook his head. "Damnest story I ever heard. What do you think Harry Ward will do with the gold coins?"

Rivera laughed. "I'm not sure. Maybe nothing. He wants to lead a simple life, just like his mentor did."

"If Harry's story is true, there's a fortune in gold coins stashed somewhere out in the Big Triangle."

"Let's keep that to ourselves. Otherwise a stampede of gold seekers will be tearing up that beautiful backcountry."

"Right. That's the last thing we need. Don't worry, even though it would make a great feature article and I'd love to write it, it'll be our secret. How's Sheriff Campbell taking his defeat?"

"Not well. He broods when he's in the office but most of the time, he's out on the golf course just like always. He still blames me for his defeat. He's sore that I didn't do anything to help him during his reelection campaign."

Carey laughed. "Why would you? He treated you like a rent car during his entire term as sheriff. The whole department is better off without him."

Rivera took a sip of iced tea and studied Carey over the rim of his glass. "So how are you and Millie getting along?"

Carey smiled. "She's a godsend—just what I needed. We've been spending some time together. Thanks for sending her my way."

"No thanks needed. I'm the one who should be thanking you. You were a huge help in breaking both of my cases."

"Glad to assist anytime. You know I love working with you on your cases. Has Gloria gone back to New Mexico yet?"

"Yeah. She left yesterday morning. I miss her already."

"You know, I remember your two previous girl-friends. Amy Rousseau and, what was the other one's name? Vivian something?"

"Vivian Ramos."

"Yeah. I remember how you were back then, first with Vivian, then with Amy. You were involved and having fun, but I've never seen you like you are now. With Gloria, your relationship seems to be at a whole new level. Trust me, Manny, a man shouldn't live alone. You'll be forty in a couple of years. Maybe Gloria's the one."

"Chris, there's no doubt in my mind. She's the one."

# 30

*Three months later.*

MANNY RIVERA SAT at his desk sipping coffee and watching snow flurries dance past his window. February was a slow time in Moab as most tourists avoided the area during the cold months. That meant things were slow for sheriff's deputies as well. He picked up the small, dark blue, velvet-covered box on his desk, flipped open the cover, and looked at the quarter-carat pear-shaped diamond ring he'd bought in Grand Junction yesterday. He rotated the box so the light would reflect from the stone's facets, reassuring himself that he'd made a good choice and hoping that Gloria would like it too. He'd find out soon enough. He was leaving in an hour for Abiquiu to visit her and propose marriage. He loved her more than he'd ever loved anyone and wanted to spend the rest of his life with her. She was fun and smart and beautiful, and spending time with her was more important to him than anything else in his life. He was sure she loved him too and hoped she'd accept his proposal. He knew modern-day couples discussed these things in a business-like way beforehand and went together to pick out the ring, but he wanted to do it the old fashion way—the way his father and grandfather had done it. Drop down on one knee, open the box containing the ring, and ask for the lady's hand in marriage.

Sheriff Louise Anderson was working out well and doing a good job despite her lack of experience in civilian law enforcement. Her only unusual management traits were her military bearing and her tendency to refer to the deputies as 'the troops'—not surprising as she had served as an officer with the Army military police for thirty years. She was a good boss, committed to serving the people and treating the staff with respect. Denny Campbell was history and wasn't missed at all. His name was rarely mentioned.

Rivera snapped the box closed and dropped it into his pocket. This was going to be a busy trip. He'd met Gloria's parents in Española, New Mexico during the Christmas holidays, but she hadn't met his parents. If she said yes to his proposal, his plan was to spend a couple of days in Las Cruces so that his parents, grandparents, siblings, cousins, and friends could meet her. No doubt, upon learning the news, his parents would organize a festive backyard barbeque, hire a mariachi band, and invite everyone Manny ever knew.

Of course, the big question was where the newlyweds would live. Gloria had once said she liked living near her parents. They were getting on in years and she was worried about them, so she visited them a couple of times a week. And Rivera had a standing job offer to go to work for Sheriff Gallegos as a Rio Arriba County deputy. All that would have to be discussed. In Rivera's mind, he would prefer living in Moab, but would live wherever it was best for Gloria.

The telephone rang just as he was standing up to leave the office. The caller was Nick Van Zandt, the coin collector from Monticello.

"Deputy Rivera, I've been debating for over a week whether or not to make this call. I finally decided it might be important."

"Yes, Mr. Van Zandt, how can I help you?"

"It's about that young man, Harry Ward, the one the newspaper said died of a rattlesnake bite out in the Big Triangle a couple of weeks ago. I understand he'd found a deep cave and was exploring it. He found some petroglyphs in there and when he dusted them off with his hand, the rattler got him."

"That's right, as best we can figure it. A herpetologist said the interior of the cave was warm enough so the rattlers in there weren't hibernating. It was a bad bite—the rattler got him on the neck. Harry made it out of the cave, staggered about a hundred feet, and collapsed. We learned about the cave from the photos in his camera and the notes in his notebook. The petroglyphs were part of a theory he was working on.

He was trying to live a minimalist life, so he had no cell phone with him—couldn't call for help. He just lay there until the venom killed him. Someone from the Center for Cosmic Consciousness found him the next day. Too bad. I liked him. He was a fine fellow."

"Yes. Well, what I wanted to tell you was that Harry brought me one of those Spanish doubloons about every other week and sold it to me—just like Peter Kennedy did."

"He did?"

"The first time, he was broke and needed some cash. We got to talking and I learned he and Peter Kennedy knew each other well, and that Harry was trying to emulate Dr. Kennedy's life. So I told him about how Peter used to sell me a coin every couple of weeks, and how we would go to my bank and get a half dozen cashier's checks made out to Peter's favorite charities. Harry asked for a list of the charities and then started doing the same thing. Every two weeks, he would bring me a coin. We'd agree on a price, go to my bank, and get a half dozen cashier's checks which he would then mail to the charities as anonymous donations. He wanted to do everything the way Dr. Kennedy did." Van Zandt laughed. "Everything except wear a pith helmet. He said that was the one thing he couldn't bring himself to do. Anyway, just thought you should know all that."

Rivera thanked Van Zandt, hung up, and thought about Harry. He missed him. Harry had adopted Dr.

Kennedy's philanthropic values as well as his professional interests, and had chosen to walk along his mentor's pathway. Like a son following in his father's footsteps.

Rivera headed south out of Moab on his five-hour drive to Abiquiu, Harry Ward still on his mind. The world had lost a good man. Rivera remembered the day they'd met and the long hike they'd shared looking for the shaman petroglyphs scraped into the rock faces over two hundred years ago by a Ute medicine man. The old Ute had hidden the white man's bad medicine far from his people so it wouldn't bring them harm. It occurred to Rivera that the Ute medicine man had been right—the gold really was bad medicine. Everyone who had taken possession of the coins after the Ute had hidden them away had died a violent death—Dr. Kennedy, Bob Livingston, and Harry Ward.

Rivera wondered how long it would be before someone else found the coins. He was certain they were well hidden—Ward would have made sure of that. Would it take months, years, or centuries? Perhaps they would never be found.

Rivera smiled, realizing he had much better things to think about than gold coins. His goal in life was to be happy, not rich. He was sure that spending the rest of his life with Gloria would make him a happy man. It was time to get started.

Made in the USA
Coppell, TX
25 January 2021

48814470R00184